Dark Curse

OPHELIA KEE

OPHELIA KEE

Cover Design by Ophelia Kee

Copyright © 2024 by Ophelia Kee

All rights reserved.

No portion of this book may be reproduced in any form without written permission from the publisher or author, except as permitted by U.S. copyright law.

To the man upon the basis of whom Flame exists.

*Some people love the nightlife and the party.
They spend their lives chasing
either the fight or the high,
but in the end,
that isn't what life truly is.
I hope PJ Sullivan finds what his heart seeks
before the night gets old.
Until then, may he always
achieve the high and enjoy the fight.
Always and Always, Boxer.
Always and Always*

Introduction to Draoithe

Draoithe Saga

Steamy hot, wickedly delicious paranormal romance, magical realism, and urban fantasy stories set in a dream to live for!

Those who come to Draoithe aid in the fight to restore the magical balance of the dream, one couple at a time.

Grab a good drink, curl up in a good seat, choose a book from the Saga, and escape into the dream while you meet the men and women who call it home.

Draoithe is a world in which myths, legends, and fairytales walk among the strange and wonderful.

They often find balance in a lifemate, and the magic from the past lives again!

Welcome to the dream...

Steamy Urban Fantasy and Paranormal Romance Stories with Fated Mates 18+ HEA! NC!

***Warning: Adult Themes, Fantasy Violence, and/or Explicit Sexual Situations. Intended for a Mature Audience.

A Note from Ophelia Kee

Note to the Reader:
A saga is defined as a long story of heroic achievement, especially a medieval prose narrative often found in Old Norse or Old Icelandic. It's a form of the novel in which the members of a social group chronicle a long story detailing a dramatic history.

Compartmentalized in several miniseries for easier reading, the Draoithe Saga tells the story of the founding of an immortal kingdom in the Leaindeail to combat those responsible for unbalancing the magic of the dream. It's told through the eyes of those connected with its creation and the readers see the story through tales of couples who find hope through their connection to Draoithe.

The central time frame is the year 2016, although pertinent information from the past reveals itself as the characters understand it. The central place is an eerily familiar yet magical realist, Tyler, Texas. As the tale draws out, other kingdoms set in other locations interact with the Druid pack to bring about the end of Peter Elliot and restore the balance of magic, so those tales, too, became a part of the Draoithe Saga as well. Cameo appearances of characters from other tales are common. Overlapping scenes from the events often relates alternate perspectives as the story unfolds.

Watch the trailer, research videos, vlogs, and more on YouTube.

Subscribe to Ophelia Kee on YouTube

Story Description

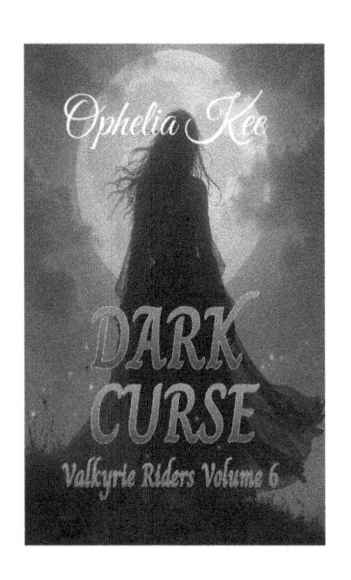

Dark Curse
Volume 6
Valkyrie Riders
A dragon knight rescues a vampire

Hannah O'Keefe was a dancer with an ancient magic. Now, she's a vampire. Following her abduction by three evil dragons, the dragon knight Flame rescues Hannah and refuses to let her fade. To survive, Hannah must embrace becoming Nightshade, a Valkyrie vampire. But she craves the sun and her former life, and being a vampire locked in a strange alternate reality and only the night is the furthest thing from the life she wanted.

Flame has loved the nightlife for centuries, but his heart aches for a Valkyrie of his own. When he finds Nightshade broken and bleeding, he knows he must protect her. But Flame harbors a dark secret which could cost him his life—and Nightshade's, too. He must help her embrace her new life before the thirst for his blood destroys her.

Can he teach her to want the cursed life she now leads and claim her for his own? Or will she fade away, leaving Flame with a broken heart for eternity?

Dark Curse by Ophelia Kee is volume six in the Valkyrie Riders Miniseries. In part one of a three part urban fantasy in which the redemption of love will either destroy the lovers or break all the rules of the dream, Nightshade wrestles with the weight of her fate and the pull of a dark attraction while Flame reveals a past more corrupt than the circumstances of her recent trauma.

It's more than a story; it's an experience. Welcome to the dream...

Urban Fantasy and Steamy Paranormal Romance with Fated Mates 18+ HEA! NC!

***Warning: Adult Themes, Fantasy Violence, and/or Explicit Sexual Situations. Intended for a Mature Audience.

Character Introduction - Nightshade

Nightshade

Hannah O'Keefe

Hannah O'Keefe was a dancer, poised on the verge of joining a dance troupe and touring the world. Her fortunes plummeted when three evil dragons abducted her, transformed her into a broken vampire, and then left her to wither in a warehouse after she failed to perform the magic they wanted. When her handsome rescuer turns out to be a dragon who refuses to let her fade, she finally realizes there is a bright light at the end of the tunnel and she might walk in the sun once more. But to do so means she must commit to becoming Nightshade, a vampire Valkyrie.

Hannah O'Keefe
AKA Nightshade
Smells like: lavender
Dance and Fitness Instructor
For the Druid Athletic Center
Mate: Flame
Red hair
Green eyes
5' 4" tall
125 lbs
24 years old
Valkyrie-vjestice vampire-den lasair-submissive

Hannah O'Keefe was born touching the well of fire, but her gift was no match for three evil dragons determined to destroy her life. It will take a lot of effort for one magnificent dragon knight to convince her to want to live the cursed life they left her.

Character Introduction - Flame

Flame

Diarmuid Cinead

Flame loved the nightlife, a good fight, good food, and beautiful women. His brothers, except Blaze, mistakenly thought he turned women into vampires to keep for himself, which almost made him give up being a dragon. His brother Blaze finally convinced him to try one last time to find his Valkyrie. He swore fealty to the Dire Wolf King.

Diarmuid Cinead
AKA Flame
Smells like: Cognac and linen
Stocks/Investment Specialist
Called by Kallik
Mate: Hannah
Auburn hair
Charcoal grey eyes
6' 5" tall
245 lbs
629 years old
Grey Dragon-Alpha

Nothing could have prepared Flame for Nightshade. She was a treasure, but damaged, dejected, and fading. Someone stripped her of her entire life, murdered her only family, and turned her into a monster. He would fight for her, die for her, and finally live, only for her.

Contents

Newsletter Friends	XIX
1. Cataloging It All	1
2. No Stronger Truth	8
3. Fade Away	15
4. Deny Her	24
5. Only Nightshade	31
6. Became Nothing More	37
7. To Breathe	44
8. Help Herself	51
9. Uncomfortable	58
10. Negate The Fact	64

11.	The Mark	70
12.	Unintelligible	76
13.	Turn Away	82
14.	An Investment	88
15.	The Room Spun	98
16.	Dancing	106
17.	More Powerful	114
18.	Collected His Thoughts	123
19.	Understood Him	131
20.	Slipped Away	137
21.	Part Of My Soul	143
22.	The Greatest Treasure	152
23.	Dark Curse	160

Sneak Peek at Dark Oath - Vampire Tears	169
Want More From The Dream?	177
Also by Ophelia Kee	181
Acknowledgments	185
Contact Ophelia Kee	186
About the Author - Ophelia Kee	187

Newsletter Friends

Magic Scroll

OPHELIA KEE

Dear Reader,
Flame and Nightshade's story is why the law must change,
why Airlea's soul returned to the dream,
and why the White Buffalo Woman will hold court at Draoithe.
The Druid pack knows none of that.

Dark Curse is Volume 6
in the Valkyrie Riders Miniseries.
I hope you enjoy it all.
For more information,
please join my group of
Newsletter Friends

Newsletter Friends

Welcome to the dream...

CHAPTER ONE
Cataloging It All

Flame

He stood, staring. The man who'd raped her writhed in pain at his feet, forgotten for the moment, inconsequential even in his agony, and nothing compared to her.

She was a vjestice vampire. Her long red hair lay limp and sweaty, but matted and tangled around her face on the dirty cot.

That alone was enough to make Flame want to send his anger in plumes of fire at her attacker. Tied face down to the cot, the thirst tormented her with the delirium of a vampire's acute hunger. Her black eyes stared at him between strands of her hair, wide with fear above pointed fangs, dripping with venom.

Flame remained frozen, lost in the vision. Flashbacks of another life tormented him before he banished them, along with his fear. His memories couldn't help her, and she was all that mattered.

Flame kicked the man he'd beaten bloody, then passed judgment on the man after he'd bitten him. Becoming a full eunuch in short order with the swipe of a razor-sharp claw and dragon flame was less than he deserved. But perhaps she could use his service.

Flame took the fool's identity along with his magic, and the man swore his oath to serve a Valkyrie for eternity. None denied a dragon who performed his duties on the orders of his king.

The man would be the dragonsworn servant to the vampire he'd brutalized for all time. It would never be enough payment for the crimes he'd perpetrated against her, but if it would help her heal, then the man would aid her.

If he failed to help her, Flame would give the man to the dawn hopefully without beating him to death first. The fool was a sacrifice already, but it remained dishonorable for a dragon to harm someone weaker than himself, no matter how angry the dragon became.

At the moment, his rage had the upper hand in the battle with his honor. She should never have been so abused.

Flame approached her carefully after ordering her servant to wait. She struggled weakly against the restraints in her attempt to get away from him. She feared him. It made his heart ache.

Flame moved slowly and whispered to her.

The last thing he wanted was for her to fear him. Considering what she'd been through, she couldn't see him as her rescuer. He probably looked like another male abuser.

She stared at him, wild-eyed. Her fear remained clear, although she seemed resigned to her fate as her restraints held her securely.

He prayed she couldn't run from him. He might never catch her if she bolted. Vampires were fast.

"I wish to assist you. Will you accept my help?"

He couldn't force anything on her. People had already forced too much on her. Flame wanted her to see him differently than those who'd harmed her. He needed to gain her trust.

Flame wanted to calm her. He couldn't tell if she had any more wounds or broken bones.

If she needed more than to feed, he needed to address it, but they needed to move swiftly.

The evil which permeated the warehouse should burn away. It made his skin crawl.

She nodded to accept help, and he reached around her to cut the restraints away from her wrists and ankles.

She breathed in deep as if sniffing in his scent. It felt sexual, but he thought it was strange behavior unless she wanted to taste him.

When she was free, and Flame had stepped back to get a blanket to cover her, her fangs extended. He laid the blanket over her and wondered.

Had she smelled his blood? Did she want to drink from him?

She didn't look like a vampire who suffered from bloodlust. Perhaps the thirst had merely taken her over the edge, and her control failed her.

He looked at the servant. She could drink from him. Flame would stop her after only a little. Just enough to quiet the thirst, and Flame would hunt for her later.

He brought the servant to her and slit his wrist with his claw and held it to her face. As soon as the smell of blood reached her, she had her fangs deep into her servant's wrist.

Her servant silently tried to pull away, and even though Flame knew the venom burned him, Flame gripped the man in place. He lived only to serve her needs.

She drank deeply. If he didn't fear the bloodlust, Flame would have allowed her to drink her fill, though it ended in her servant's death.

How long had she gone without feeding? Far too long.

He couldn't allow further harm to come to her. After two minutes, he forcefully separated the servant's wrist from her fangs. He let the dragon flames seal the servant's wrist injury before he pushed the servant away from her.

Flame watched her. She lay still, too afraid to move much more than her eyes. The vampire lifted one hand and tried to brush the loose strands of hair from her face. She missed and sighed as she allowed her hand to fall back to the cot, too weak to try again.

Flame was too afraid of the blood lust to give her more blood to combat her weakness. It should have helped more than it did. Perhaps there was something else wrong.

"I'm Flame. Will you tell me your name?"

She was Nightshade to him, but he wanted her human name, to hear her speak to him. He wanted to learn about her.

"Hannah O'Keefe."

She whispered it before she closed her eyes. Her voice carried the signature soft, slurred tones of the vampire. It drew him in.

The siren song of the vampire was irresistible to Flame. Something about vampires excited him, as no other ever had.

She was from the kingdom of Munster? Wait, it no longer existed. Was it still possible the women of her lineage remained den lasair?

She had the hair for it and the right last name. It fit that her family's lion represented deathless courage as she was now a vampire.

Did she even know of her possible heritage? He studied her aura. The flame was present. Nightshade could command the fire from the well.

She was beautiful in the way all true Gaelic Irish women were. Clear skin made more creamy white by her vampiric state. Freckles lay sprinkled across her cheeks and the bridge of her nose.

Flame knew she was his mate, but he hadn't been prepared for the level of intensity looking upon her stirred his feelings. He'd never felt desire for a woman so keenly as he felt it for this one. And she was a vampire.

It couldn't have gotten any more complicated. It didn't matter. She was for him. He would deal with the rest later.

Hannah made it difficult for him to think. She was in no condition to view him as a suitor.

He had to move her out of the vile warehouse he found her in. He needed to finish the mission.

Flame would have time to figure out what to do when they were safe and far away. Her safety and current physical comfort were all he needed to handle at the moment. He could manage it.

He didn't need to know how her skin felt or how her hair smelled. But he couldn't stop himself from cataloging it all, anyway.

CHAPTER TWO

No Stronger Truth

Flame

"I need to carry you from here. I need to get you away to someplace safe and comfortable. Will you permit me to lift you and move you from here?"

She wouldn't be walking out. Flame wanted to beg her, but it was inappropriate behavior.

His singular desire to help vampires, especially beautiful red-headed ones, got tamped down. His raging need to help his mate was harder to tame, but the last thing he needed was his brothers' scrutiny.

It was bad enough when Ash had found him working for the vjestice of an enclave in Romania, hunting down rogue vampires there about a hundred years ago. He'd learned and stayed to help them with a minor to gain knowledge.

Ash never asked, and Flame never explained. He was only glad he'd sent Flare away before Ash caught up with him.

"Please, don't let them find me," she pleaded.

Hannah had the soft drawl common in vampire speech which accompanied their allure. She wasn't actively drawing him in. Still, she was beyond sexy.

Who were they? Why did she hope to avoid them? Who chased his treasure?

Flame's anger rose. None would take her from him! She was his treasure. He found her. Only a fool attempted to steal from a dragon.

"Who's looking for you?"

Flame needed to know if there was a threat. He would eliminate any threat to her. She was to be protected at all costs. Dying would be worth it, so long as she remained safe.

"The ones like you."

Her words barely whispered, and her energy faded.

What did she mean, like himself? Did she mean other dragons? Was she concerned about his brothers? It made little sense.

Did she know other dragons? Did she even know he was a dragon? How? Why would she be afraid of them if she knew them? Too many questions for later.

He gently turned her body, wrapped the blanket around her, and lifted her into his arms. She weighed nothing, further angering him.

He settled her head against his chest and his biceps, so she couldn't fall. Flame met up with his brothers, Luke, and Javier.

When they were ready, Luke gave the orders, and they left the warehouse burning behind them. The evil would become ashes in the breeze.

They did a repeat performance of the warehouse they'd taken first and headed to the safe house, crowded into the vans in short order. Once there, Luke gave more orders.

The shifters all ate. Magic required energy. Flame followed his orders without tasting his food, but his attention never strayed from the beautiful vampire.

Flame had difficulty concentrating on anything but Hannah. He got a nightgown on her slender frame and wrapped her back in the blanket.

DARK CURSE

She was frail, too weak, and not healing. He feared she'd gone into shock. She might fade.

The thought damn near panicked him. He pushed it away and concentrated on assessing what he knew.

Drinking from the servant hadn't seemed to help her much. The thirst still rode her hard. She needed blood. She needed to feed.

Flame worried. Her eyes were black, but she wasn't in her vampire guise.

He didn't believe she'd always had black eyes. Something was seriously wrong.

Locked to another, her situation angered him further. It wasn't a proper lock, otherwise she would've been safe from her rapist. That hadn't been the case. It gave him hope.

He had to put the images out of his mind, or the servant would get a second beating.

Flame and his brother Blaze had done a lot of research into sedr and veritas magic. They wanted to understand how dragon magic functioned and mutated to create vampires.

Hannah's black eye color looked more like that of a locked shifter mate in their more formidable animal state. She wasn't a shifter.

Someone locked her somehow, but what was the lock for? Could he break it?

If she wasn't locked sexually, then what had happened to her? He chewed on all the questions his observations led to. He had far more questions than he had answers.

Flame needed to get her some place safe and quiet, so he could think it out and discover how to help her.

When Luke gave the order to vacate the safe house, Flame couldn't have been happier to leave. The sooner he could get her to some place safer, the sooner he could figure out the situation and implement solutions.

They arrived at the dragons' temporary residence more than an hour before dawn. Flame carried his treasure into his bedroom. He kicked the door closed behind him after ordering Hannah's man to guard the door.

With no name left to him and part of his soul stolen with it, Flame named the servant after the woman he served.

Flame's dragon nature wanted to hoard Hannah away from the world. He wasn't in the mood to fight himself.

The servant was despicable and shouldn't be too close to his mistress until Flame had better control. Guarding her door against anyone who might molest her peace was the best place for him.

The room was dark. Technically, it wasn't a bedroom. Someone had designed it as a small media room or maybe a large office area. It had no windows.

Flame had no opposition from the others when he claimed the room for his dragon lair. In retrospect, it seemed fortuitous.

No windows equaled no danger to Nightshade. The sun wouldn't reach her to take her from him.

The room had two enormous wardrobes, two large chests of drawers, two nice armchairs, a small table, two nightstands with lamps on either side of the king-size bed, and a full-length mirror mounted to the wall. It felt comfortable.

He placed her gently on the bed. She was awake again. Flame saw her quietly looking at him. The sun wouldn't call her to sleep for more than an hour.

He thought his report into the telepathic link he shared with his brothers, so Ash could handle Luke while Flame watched over his treasure.

Hannah is too weak to hunt. She needs to feed before she sleeps. I'll hunt for her and return shortly. When the sun rises, she'll sleep. She is den lasair and vjestice vampire.

I'll report it. Luke's orders remain. Care for your Valkyrie until a new mission arises. We swear our oaths tonight after sunset.

Thanks, Ash.

"I need to hunt for you, so you can feed before you sleep. Stay here and rest. I won't be gone long. No one will disturb you."

She nodded her understanding, and Flame left to find a couple of deer to borrow some life force from. In vino veritas. In wine was the truth, and in blood was the magic. For vampires, there was no stronger truth.

CHAPTER THREE

Fade Away

Hannah

She was so thirsty. She'd been in the warehouse for three days. For three nights, the men tormented and used her monstrously, but she would wake up completely healed each afternoon.

It was the fourth night, and she could no longer think clearly. Hannah needed to drink. It sickened her how crazed she felt.

Confused when the pain in her rectum eased, maybe they finished torturing her.

She opened her eyes, and her fear overwhelmed her. She tried to move away from the charcoal grey gaze of the man who faced her.

He was powerful, and his aura was large and overt. He scared her more than the other three had frightened her combined.

She lay still, barely breathing, when she realized once again she lacked the strength to escape her bonds.

The man, who'd begun the assault on her, cowered at the big man's feet. He no longer acted so powerful.

Faced with the overt alpha male, Hannah knew she'd met her death. It would finally all end.

"I wish to assist you. Will you accept my help?"

He hadn't come to kill her, but to rescue her? His words startled her.

What choice did she have? Fighting a man like him was pointless. She had learned the hard way.

She nodded. He reached around her to cut away her restraints. She couldn't help herself.

She breathed in his crisp, sharp scent of cognac and linen. He was like the other three, but so much richer. Her fangs descended. She needed to feed.

The man had what she needed. If she could drink from him, the thirst would fade. The thirst drove her mad. She wanted only a taste.

He studied her for a moment. Then he yanked the cowering man to his feet and sliced open his wrist. He offered it to her, and even though the cowering man struggled against it, the powerful man ignored him.

She couldn't refuse. She needed blood. It wouldn't stop the thirst, only keep her from dying. She drank.

Hannah hated herself. She was so disgusted with what had happened. It shouldn't be.

She was *den lasair*. She still had trouble accepting that she was a vampire. Hannah certainly had never asked, nor had she wanted to be one.

Drinking the blood made her feel unclean as much as the rape made her feel dirty. Her life felt ugly and unclean. Self-preservation was all that remained, and she no longer believed that instinct held any power.

Her life had flipped upside down two weeks before. All she'd wanted was to dance.

That man should've burned, but her fire didn't touch him. She blocked it from her mind as she drank. She was too weak to deal with it.

Hannah needed more blood. It gave her more strength, but the thirst still pressed her. She needed the big man's blood.

She lay still. Even with blood, she remained too weak to move much more than her eyes.

She lifted one hand and tried to brush the loose strands of hair from her face. Hannah missed and sighed. She needed a lot more to drink if she were to heal and move.

"I'm Flame. Will you tell me your name?"

"Hannah O'Keefe," she whispered.

She closed her eyes as fear over revealing her name gripped her. Would he use his knowledge against her? Maybe she would do better to stay silent.

He seemed excited about her name. Maybe he liked it and wouldn't mistreat her.

Had someone sent him to find her? Her aunt maybe. Where she would have gotten the money was anyone's guess.

The man sure as hell wasn't excited about the way she looked. She couldn't have been less attractive.

She felt his fingers move the offending strands of hair away from her face behind her ear. He was warm, and she felt so cold.

The others had done something to her. She could no longer touch the fire she'd been born to wield. She lacked the strength to mourn it, though.

When his finger traced the skin on her face, it felt strangely erotic. Hannah wanted to laugh at the absurdity of her thoughts. Maybe she had lost her mind.

Warm fingers equaled erotic? It was laughable.

"I need to carry you from here to get you someplace safe and comfortable. Will you permit me to lift you and move you from here?"

He asked if he could carry her away? Did he seek her permission?

He surprised her. No one had considered what she wanted for the last two weeks. For a moment, her puzzlement grew. Was it some sort of trick?

No matter. Anywhere was better than where she was. She would go with him. It wasn't as if she could stop him if he took her.

"Please, but don't let them find me."

If she only had to deal with one instead of three, maybe she could get away from him. She only wanted a quiet place to rest and think. Then perhaps she could learn what to do, how to get home.

She wanted her life back. She wanted to see her aunt and dance. And never drink blood again.

"Who's looking for you?"

He seemed not to know. Maybe she had a chance. Maybe he didn't know the other three.

She watched his face, but it gave nothing away.

"The ones like you."

Her energy was gone. He sensed it and asked nothing else from her. Whatever he was, the others were definitely the same.

Flame gently turned her body, wrapped the blanket around her, and lifted her into his arms.

The sight of him seeing her naked should have embarrassed Hannah, but she was too weak. He covered her, which Hannah appreciated, because it allowed her to keep at least a small portion of her dignity.

He settled her head against his chest and his biceps so she couldn't fall. Flame was all hard muscle, but he felt good, warm. He probably had a fire like the others, too.

He was careful not to jar or rattle her. Flame seemed different that way, kind.

The smell of cognac and linen returned, relaxing her.

The man she'd fed from followed them meekly.

All hope of escaping died in her when they met up with other men. Some were like Flame, a few were different, but all enormously more powerful than she was.

At least the three who had taken her weren't among them. One man gave the orders, and they left the warehouses burning behind them. She wasn't sad to watch them burn.

It was a quick ride to a house in the suburbs. Flame eased her into a nightgown. Taking care not to hurt her or allow anyone else to see her nudity.

It felt good to be clothed. When was the last time she'd worn clothing? Fourteen days? Sixteen days?

She didn't know. It seemed like a million-dollar luxury. One nightgown equaled a slice of her dignity. She appreciated the gesture immensely.

Flame cared for her as if she had a grand worth and deserved it. She wanted to be valuable.

He covered her in the blanket again, and she slipped away, overcome by the intensity of her emotions.

Was she asleep, or merely lost in her nightmare? She didn't know, but awareness of the surrounding environment had faded, at least for a while.

When she had an awareness of her surroundings again, Flame carried her into a different house, with the same man still following him like a lost puppy. He gave instructions to the man, but Hannah couldn't focus well enough to understand.

He stepped into a windowless bedroom and kicked the door closed behind him. The room smelled intensely of cognac and linen.

Flame had brought her to his personal space. She was in his bedroom. Hanna knew she should have panicked, but it took energy she didn't possess.

He laid her gently on the bed. She didn't move. She just looked at him.

Hannah feared her torture would begin again. He had her alone.

Whoever Flame was, he had enough power to take from her whatever he wanted. She couldn't stop him. She just hoped he would be quick and tire of her soon or help her find mercy.

"I need to hunt for you so you can feed before you sleep, so I need you to stay here and rest. I won't be gone long. No one will disturb you."

She nodded, still in despair. He wanted to keep her alive.

Flame seemed kind though. He hadn't hurt her. He even understood her need for blood. Flame hunted for blood for her, but his words would keep her locked in the room until he returned.

What chance did she have against him or those others, anyway? Her fire no longer came at her command. It didn't work against men like him. She was too weak to walk. The dawn would come soon.

She was still a prisoner at the mercy of Flame instead of the three nameless ones. She was nothing but a toy for them to amuse themselves.

Her tears fell, red blood-filled tears. They stained the bedclothes, but she didn't have the strength to deal with that, either.

Maybe he'd kill her for it, and everything would all end. The abuse, torture, and rape had exhausted her. Death might be easier.

Hannah had never been a quitter, but in her exhaustion, her despair gripped her hard. She wanted to fade away.

CHAPTER FOUR
Deny Her

Flame

He returned to the house with two pitchers of deer blood. Flame placed one in the refrigerator, grabbed a glass, and carried the other to his room.

He'd only been gone for half an hour. He still had time to help her. If she drank before sunrise, she would have the strength to heal in her sleep. Hannah was immortal. Rest and food would help her.

Flame entered the room. Awake, Hannah stared listlessly at the door, but he doubted she saw him. Tears stained her face. It wrenched his heart.

Why did she cry? Was she afraid of him?

He feared the worst when she didn't move. He'd watched a vampire die from the fade once. It had taken a long time. Maybe months.

The vampires's consort had died, and he ceased to move. Eventually, the enclave gave up and left him for the dawn to take him.

Flame went straight to Hannah. He sat down on the bed next to her, wanting to pick her up and hold her, but he feared she'd see his desperation to help her for what else it was.

Desperate to touch her again when smelling the lavender in the room reminded him of the way her hair smelled.

Flame had a thing for vampires. He knew it. He didn't bother lying to himself.

Her red hair tempted him, too. She couldn't have been more of his fantasy brought to life if he'd crafted her himself.

"Why do you cry?"

Flame would move the stars around in the night sky if the beautiful redhead on his bed would smile a little.

"I wish to be free. I want to leave."

She whispered it as if she feared reprisal from him. Hannah feared him, but her desire was so great it overcame her fear.

She voiced the truth of her heart. She desired to leave. Did she wish to leave him, the room, the house, Texas? He wasn't sure.

"Where would you go? I will take you."

Flame felt compelled to help her, even if it meant he gave her up.

Luke had granted all the women sanctuary, but he'd never allowed them to become prisoners again. Flame didn't even care. He just wanted to ease whatever suffering caused her tears.

If leaving would do it, then he would help her. He would deny her nothing. If she wanted to go to Moscow, he would take her.

Hannah froze and blinked her red-rimmed black eyes several times. His response wasn't what she'd expected.

"You'd set me free?"

"If that's your wish, then yes. You have sanctuary here, and my orders are to see to your comfort and well-being. If that means you need to leave, then it's my job to see you to where you wish to be, safely. Where do you need to go? I'll take you."

Flame reiterated his desire to obey her wishes on the matter.

He didn't want her to go anywhere, but he wouldn't be a kidnapper. Flame couldn't keep her captive. He was serious when he offered to help her leave.

Hannah thought for a moment, then she seemed to decide. He could almost see her decide to take the risk of trusting him a bit.

"Flame, where am I?"

Flame almost smiled at her question. She said his name, and his heart sang. He felt silly, like a young boy who finally got noticed by his crush. It was ridiculous and true.

"We are right outside of Tyler, TX."

Flame spoke the truth because she wasn't a captive and knowing where he'd brought her would help her. It took some of the fear away.

He needed to take her fear away. She shouldn't be afraid of him. Hannah was everything.

"The sun will rise soon. I can't get there in time."

Hannah seemed frustrated.

Flame knew she was too weak to travel anywhere. Maybe thinking she could travel helped her.

He poured the glass full from the pitcher and offered it to her. She struggled to rise to take it.

He set it on the nightstand and eased her to a half-sitting position. She took the glass from him then.

It shook, so he reached to steady it for her to drink. When she finished it, her eyes slipped closed, exhausted.

"Hannah, will you stay and sleep? If you still wish to leave when you wake, we can arrange it."

He barely kept the break out of his voice. He didn't want to arrange anything which took her away from him.

If she left, he'd go with her. Even if it meant he was an oath breaker.

He needed her. The dragon inside demanded he keep her close, protect her, and give her what she needed.

"These are your quarters. You sleep here."

Hannah made the statement feel slightly like a question in her breathy, vampire voice.

Flame almost shivered as her voice washed over him. How long had it been since he'd been around a vampire? Maybe a hundred years until he'd seen Mihaela and Andrei. Perhaps that was why her voice got to him.

He thought he'd overcome it. Hearing her speech was like pure bliss. The scales of his sleeping dragon lay down flat in pleasure.

"Yes. Would you prefer I leave?"

Flame would sleep on the other side of the door if she ordered him out, but he wouldn't admit he couldn't leave her.

His orders were to see to her well-being. How follow that command if he couldn't see her?

"No. The thirst weighs on me heavily. I can smell it on you. You're like they are. I'm disgusted with myself for asking. You knew at the warehouse. Please, I need your blood. Can we make a trade of some sort?"

Flame sat in the chair heavily. He knew what she wanted from him.

He closed his eyes and felt the fangs sink into his wrist. The pain was momentary. The fangs were sharp like needles, and the venom burned like acid.

Clara pulled the blood from his body, and he came. Flame shook his head to end the dream. Or was it a nightmare? He didn't know anymore. The memories haunted him still.

"It was obvious, but it would only have been so to me. I've studied the vampire rather extensively. I don't know if I can give you what you request, but I certainly couldn't trade you for it."

Flame didn't hide the quaver in his voice. His desire to give her what she wanted was too strong. She was his mate and denying her felt so incredibly wrong. Bleeding for her wasn't a good idea. It could be his demise.

He feared her. Flame had avoided vampires in any intimate setting for five centuries, even though they'd driven nearly a lifetime of research and study. He wasn't strong enough for what she would say next.

Flame had to think, but his head was in a daze. He was tired. Would he be able to look at himself in the mirror tomorrow? The answer was 'no'.

Would he deny her request?

CHAPTER FIVE
Only Nightshade

Flame

Again, the answer was 'no'. It was wrong.

He knew the penalty if he got caught. No dragon could bleed for any but the Valkyrie or life and death. The penalty for bleeding for a vampire was always death.

She was his identified lifemate, but he needed to turn her before she would be his Valkyrie. The thirst wouldn't kill her, but her suffering might kill him.

"Please, Flame. You're like them. I know it will work. I'll give you anything you desire. Please, just take the thirst away from me."

Hannah was weak, and the thirst made her crazy. Flame knew she wouldn't die from it, but she was desperate.

How could he help her if she was delirious from the thirst? Had it ever really been a question? Most already viewed his honor as worthless. He had his orders.

"Shoe size?"

Hannah blinked.

"Eight."

"What size are your pants?"

Flame asked her another question. He had a pen and a notepad. He needed to write it down for Smoke and Ash to get the information for the personal shoppers.

She needed clothes and shoes. So he demanded information from her, then he'd bleed for her.

She answered him as he barked questions at her about dress size, bra size, and panty size. Flame had never been so hard from hearing a woman's panty size. It was madness, what he did.

He should tell her 'no' and find another solution, but he couldn't deny her what she asked of him.

She was his lifemate. He was a shifter.

Damn it! He fucking wanted it, too.

Flame gave the sizes along with his color preferences of black, white, grey, and sage green to the servant in the hall, with orders to sleep when the sun rose.

Flame wouldn't leave. He would keep her safe in his arms while she slept.

He would trade her for his blood. The coercion of the innocent could be damned.

She asked him, not the other way around. It wasn't as if he'd demanded she agree to be his Valkyrie. He didn't want a thrall.

"Please, Flame. Please, I'm begging you. I'll do anything you ask."

He loved to hear a beautiful woman beg. Her low, sultry voice soothed him. It raised the gooseflesh on his skin.

Her presence in the room overwhelmed his senses. Holding her would ease the dragon.

"Let me hold you while you sleep. Please?"

He asked her as he stripped off his clothes, leaving his undershirt and boxers. Hannah watched him undress, and she nodded immediately.

Desperate to agree and taste him, he was as desperate to hold her in his arms while she drank from him. He was so screwed.

Flame didn't bother hiding his desire from her. The thirst had taken her. She would remember later, but it didn't matter.

He could've requested any sexual act, any perverted fantasy, and she would have agreed. He only wanted to hold her close, to know she was safe. To feel her warmth next to him.

He would fulfill his desire at her expense, but the thirst was too strong for her to care. Flame would cum, and things would be messy and difficult when they woke later.

Hannah was redemption. Flame was too weak not to claim it for himself.

This time, things would be different. Blaze had convinced him. It had better be different.

Flame approached her on the bed. She feared him. He was new and obviously in control. She waited for him to lie next to her.

He turned her body gently, so she didn't panic. He put his arms around her and tilted his head slightly so she could bite him on the neck where the vein was close to the surface.

"I only want to hold you while you sleep, so you'll be safe. Don't fear harming me. Drink your fill, but know I'll never allow it, except just before dawn."

Flame knew it was wrong. Feeding her and offering to do it every morning at dawn was so wrong. No vampire ever said 'no' to dragon blood. She wouldn't leave him as long as she could drink from him.

He had to make her want to stay with him meaningfully before she realized what he'd done. That level of coercion on his part could see him executed again. He was already in too deep. There was no way he wouldn't follow through.

All thoughts vanished as the needle-like hollow fangs pierced his neck. His hard cock throbbed against her, but she seemed unaware. She was only intent on ending her thirst, drinking his blood. He had her full attention.

Flame wanted to scream in agony as the venom burned into his veins. It was far worse at the neck than it had been at the wrist. He only hissed at the pain.

Invented images of Clara and Joselle turning to ash in the sun mocked him. He held Hannah tighter to him. Nothing would take her from him.

Her breasts pressed against his chest. Not this time. Not this one.

Her scent of lavender tickled his nose. He would never leave her for another to torture and ruin. He would protect her. She would never be ash. She was everything.

Hannah pulled the blood from his body, and he came so hard he cried her name in a harsh whisper. Then he did the unthinkable.

He begged her not to stop. She didn't. The euphoric bliss was so high he might never come down.

The sun claimed her for sleep before she stopped drinking from him. He felt the sickening withdrawal of her fangs as they slowly receded. Then the wound on his neck healed.

As it was dawn, and he'd stolen the sexual energy from her feeding, Flame regenerated. He had no scar. There would be no obvious signs.

Flame didn't move. He held Hannah close to his chest. He needed to sleep, but the euphoric high was slow to fade.

He'd found his lifemate, and she was, without a doubt, the sexiest creature alive. She was den lasair and vjestice vampire, and she had a serious taste for him.

He was so fucking screwed. But it didn't matter at that moment. It would never matter. She was his greatest treasure. Only Nightshade would ever matter.

CHAPTER SIX
Became Nothing More

Hannah

It was late afternoon, maybe three o'clock, when she woke. Everything smelled of cognac and linen, even her breath.

She wanted to groan out loud. It hadn't been a strange dream. The thirst was gone. It had never been missing before. Hannah frowned.

She'd drunk from him, and oh, what had she done? He'd been so aroused. He sternly warned her he would only allow it at dawn. After she bit him in the sexiest voice she'd ever heard, he begged her not to stop. She shivered with the memory of the power she seemed to have over him.

Hannah blushed as she recalled the way his hard chest felt as he tightened his hold on her with powerful arms. Flames danced over them both when she shivered.

The warmth and tingle of the flames were fantastic. She wanted to hold the purple and black flame in her fingers as she had as a child.

The red flames didn't come at her call anymore, but she wouldn't deny herself the pleasure of the purple and black ones.

She missed the flames. They were not the beautiful red she was familiar with, but they were warm and comforting.

Hannah had wanted to cry when her connection to the well had been severed. The three men had mocked her, laughing at her. They had the flame. They showed it to her, but they didn't let her touch it.

As close as she could get to it was when they lit their members on fire and forced her to douse the fire in her mouth. It didn't burn, but they had seemed to enjoy abusing her that way. Their fire had been purple and black, too.

Flame was like them. He had a purple and black fire. He gave it to her freely, though. Sure, he was asleep, but it was still in response to her shivering.

Flame was different. Hannah could feel his strength, but he was kind. He'd asked only a seemingly insignificant request of her. She would've done anything. Flame begged only to hold her while she slept.

He smelled good. He tasted good. Flame had been careful with her. When the thirst had overtaken her, and she'd offered him anything he wanted in exchange for a taste of his blood, he demanded her clothing sizes and to hold her.

He could have taken anything he wanted from her, but he didn't. He took nothing, only gave himself to her.

The others had let her beg for hours while they took turns raping her. When they finished, they would only slit their wrist and let the blood drip onto her lips. It had never been enough. The thirst had never died away as it was now. She felt almost... normal.

Hannah had clothes, food, and warmth for the first time in weeks. It might not seem like much to others, but it mattered to her.

Nothing hurt, and she was reasonably comfortable, even if Flame held her a bit too tightly. Being in his arms felt nice. For the first time in a long while, she felt like a real person.

She could smell the blood in the pitcher, but it wouldn't be as satisfying as Flame's blood.

What kind of man had purple and black flames, and the power to steal her flames from her? Could Flame give the fire back to her?

The three nameless ones had laughed at her, saying she would never have her flame again. Did they speak the truth? Was it gone forever?

Flame was larger than any of the nameless men who'd kidnapped her and damaged her. He was far more powerful than any of them. She could still feel the magic in others, at least.

Could he undo what had happened to her? Could she take the risk of trusting him enough to find out? What would he want in exchange if it was possible?

Flame already knew the thirst would claim her again, eventually. He'd even hinted she could drink from him every day, but only before dawn. If he waited long enough, she would beg him to do anything he wanted if he would only give her a taste. She was worse than a heroin or crack addict.

Well, not exactly. She wouldn't beg anyone. Just the ones who had whatever Flame had.

What was he? She didn't know, but she could smell it. It was reptilian.

Come to think of it, Flame seemed to have a lot of knowledge about her, and she had too little about him, except that he had a thing for being consumed alive by another.

That was creepy. He'd acted kindly to her. He was attractive, but wishing to be swallowed alive was a huge turnoff.

Who was she kidding? She couldn't call him creepy without recognizing she burned to consume him alive, and she'd drowned in the euphoria of drinking from him at dawn.

Hell, she wanted to do it again, but she didn't wish to anger him and make him cut her off. She was as creepy, wanting his blood as he was, desiring to give it to her.

Hannah hated her thoughts. They disgusted her. She didn't want to drink from him.

She wanted to leave, did she not? He had said she could go. He would plan to take her anywhere she wanted to go.

She could go home and rebuild her life. What would she do about the thirst?

She'd been too weak to travel before. Hannah could travel tonight, though. She should go to Houston and resume her life.

Her aunt would help her. She was old now, but still smart. Together, they would find some way.

Hannah could take Flame with her. He could let her have a taste every morning. No one had to know. Her friends would all think she was on some new fad diet and leave her alone.

No. The fantasy should have ended to resume her life. Flame wouldn't go with her to be a blood donor. The entire idea was a ridiculous fever dream.

She wanted to rail at the universe. The movies always made being a vampire seem sexy. It was a torturous madness. Leave it to Hollywood to turn a horrible thing into a romantic interlude.

Cognac and linen were suddenly the most intoxicating and dangerous scents on the planet. It surrounded Hannah and danced as beautiful warm flames over her skin, which tingled as they hopped and touched.

She breathed it into her soul with each breath, and she had drunk it down until she had drowned in it at dawn. She had to have it again.

Hannah was a realist. She would stay with Flame if he offered to let her drink from him because he tasted divine and because she feared facing the alternative. She feared the thirst and the hold it had over her.

Hannah feared the depths of depravity she might sink to make it subside. Most of all, she feared others like Flame finding her and abusing her again.

Worse, she feared the sun. How the hell could she live in the dark forever?

Worst of all, Hannah feared she would never touch her precious flame or ever dance again. She became nothing more than breathing anxiety.

CHAPTER SEVEN

To Breathe

Hannah

Something was wrong with her. Hannah would never know the love of a man, the comfort of a family. She was a vampire. She knew it, but accepting it was more than she could handle.

She'd concentrated her time on her dancing in college. The right man had never approached her.

Her aunt had always laughingly told her if she set the standard too high, she would die alone. It now seemed infinitely more likely her aunt had been right.

What had they done to her? The fools at the warehouse even complained they couldn't use her properly. That hadn't stopped them, but none had taken her that way.

She was still as intact as she'd ever been. As silly as it was, as if she didn't have enough to think about, she couldn't stop thinking about never finding love.

Hannah was far from being able to worry about seeking a lover, and perhaps her virginity was the least of her problems. But her tortured mind latched onto her fears and held them close.

She was only twenty-four. She felt as if men should still appeal to her on some level, maybe in some bright future where she was no longer cursed five ways from Sunday.

As damaged as she was. It could never happen. No bright future existed because whenever any of them ordered her to do something, she complied immediately. She didn't struggle or run. She went along with it.

Hannah could see other ways, but had no will to fight back. It was disconcerting.

How could she fix that? She couldn't submit to everything. Life would be impossible.

Hannah needed a shower. She felt grimy. She needed to wash away the stench of the warehouse. Maybe when Flame woke up, he would allow her to bathe.

Being clean would be nice. She wanted to wash off the smell of stale sex and evil use. If she no longer smelled like the warehouse, maybe she could think differently, see a better future.

The debt she owed would only grow worse as time passed. Flame said she had a sanctuary. Hannah hoped it included a change of clothes and a hot bath.

She would need to ask him for a shirt or something. She owed Flame too much already, but naked wasn't an option.

The real question was, what was the price for all of it? She had no money. What would he demand as payment?

"Are you awake, Hannah?"

She heard him whisper. He was awake.

She nodded. She was afraid to speak to him.

While Flame slept, he seemed safe. Awake, he was the powerful alpha male who'd allowed her to drink her fill and demanded she not stop.

He'd also warned her not to bother him about it, except at dawn. Hannah feared him, and because she was desperate for another taste of him, the last thing she wanted was to anger him.

"I'm afraid we both need to bathe. Will you come with me?"

He asked her, but he had included her in his needs.

She had no choice but to agree to his wishes. She wanted the simple pleasure of a bath and was desperate for a bit of a soak, but having no choice made the idea less pleasant.

"I don't have clothes, Flame. Do you think I could borrow something?"

He shifted, so he loosened his hold on her, and he could see her eyes. She instantly missed the warmth of his too-tight embrace.

"You have clothes. I arranged for you to be comfortable. Would you like to see them so you can choose something?"

He did what? How had he managed it? Why? She nodded, still too afraid to speak much.

He let go of her with a sigh and let the fire wink out. Hannah almost wanted to cry, but she held it together.

Not that it would have mattered. The blood and other fluids had already ruined the bedclothes. She wondered if anyone would notice her tears amidst the chaos. She just didn't want to appear as weak and broken.

Flame rose and held his hand out for her to rise with him. She stood up, unsteady at first, but none the worse for wear. They walked to a wardrobe, and he pulled open the doors.

Women's clothes crammed the chest. All in her size and all expensive name brands. He opened the chest, and Hannah found it filled with undergarments, socks, nightwear, and anything that didn't hang.

Flame caught her before she collapsed from the anxiety attack. He held her close to him as she trembled. He planned on keeping her.

The last thing she wanted was to be a pet. The fire spread over them again.

He petted her head and whispered to her until she regained herself. She would figure a way out, but it didn't stop her from taking comfort in his arms, in the warmth of his fire.

She felt twisted and torn inside. He seemed so kind. Maybe he was different, but would she ever be free as she once had been?

"Flame, where did all those clothes come from?"

She forgot herself and asked. Hannah cringed and waited for the blow that didn't come. He didn't hit her. He simply answered her as if she had a right to know.

"I bought them from the mall. I paid a personal shopper to coordinate them in your size while you slept. Smoke and Ash generously made the trip to pick them up. Your servant hung them for you about three hours ago while you slept."

Flame left out no detail. He seemed concerned about her panic attack, and he wanted her to have all the information so he could stop another one. He wasn't angry with her.

Surprise washed over Hannah. He hadn't berated her or lashed out at her for questioning him. She took a chance then and asked another question.

"You bought them?"

She shook her head before he answered the dumb question.

"I owe you a fortune. I can't afford this."

Flame laughed out loud. His amusement sounded genuine. Why?

She waited for him to speak. What was so funny? Was he laughing at her?

"Hannah, I don't want repayment. I bought them because you needed them. As a dragon, I don't need any money."

He grinned at her as if his explanation made sense. If the man was crazy enough to not want money, then Hannah would have to take advantage of him.

It was better than wearing her stained nightgown forever, and even that was a gift from him. Hannah accepted his offering with no grace, but she accepted it.

"Okay. Okay."

She tried to breathe.

CHAPTER EIGHT
Help Herself

*H*annah
There were thousands of dollars in clothes hanging in the wardrobe alone. She wouldn't think about the bras and panties.

If he didn't want the money back, then he only wanted one thing. She couldn't give it to him. Things would go badly when he realized it. She dreaded the outcome. Then she remembered his words.

"Wait. Did you say 'my servant' hung these? I don't have any servants. I'm a dancer, and I just finished dance school. There's no money for servants."

She felt like she was at the funhouse in the hall of mirrors, where everything appeared distorted. She'd escaped a nightmare to land in the Twilight Zone.

Hannah forgot herself for a moment, and she was a dance school graduate again. Soon she would join a dance troupe and travel the world. It was all she wanted. It was what she'd spent her life working toward.

"Hannah's man is a gift to you. He's a dragonsworn servant. You don't have to keep him. If you don't want him, I'll turn him to ash. He was worthless before. His only hope lies in you finding some chores for him."

Flame tried explaining, but she was no longer sure he spoke in English. What was dragonsworn?

Turning someone to ash seemed extreme, even if they were worthless. Flame seemed serious.

The last thing she wanted was to anger him or have him ridicule her.

"I don't understand."

Hannah wasn't stupid, but none of it made sense to her. She lowered her head. She waited for him to hit her and tell her how dumb she was. The blow didn't come.

When she dared to look at his face again, he frowned in thought. He wasn't frowning at her.

DARK CURSE

When he had sufficient control over himself, he looked at her again.

"I will help you understand, okay? I won't hit you. No one here will hurt you. Hannah, you're safe. I'm not like those other men. I need to keep you safe, and I won't allow anyone to touch you or harm you."

He spoke to her as an adult spoke to a frightened child. He acted as if he didn't expect her to believe him, which she didn't, but he seemed upset she wouldn't.

Flame blew out his breath and let his anger go. He walked to the other chest and took a cell phone from the charger. He handed it to her.

"Open it. Text Hannah's man to come to the room."

Her hand shook, but she opened the phone, scrolled through the contacts, and sent the text as he instructed.

Flame waited. There was a knock at the door. He told them to enter. A man came through the door with his head lowered.

"My lady, how may I serve you?"

The man asked without looking at her.

"Look up at me, Hannah's man. Let the lady see your face, but don't look at her."

Flame ordered the man.

Hannah stepped back. It was the man who had followed Flame from the warehouse, but he seemed different. What had Flame done to him?

"I'm a dragon knight. I'm a protector of the realm. He broke the law of the Ri ruirech in his near presence. Where the king walks, his realm exists. I caught this man performing a criminal act, so I required no witnesses or testimony. I judged him guilty of forcing himself on a woman without her consent. He's a eunuch, sentenced to eternal service to pay for his crimes. Will you accept him as your loyal servant? If you say 'no', I'll end his existence instead."

"He's a unicorn?"

Hannah was confused and frightened. She didn't like the servant guy, but she feared Flame. He was powerful. She was upset, making it difficult to think or breathe.

Flame chuckled and shook his head. The sound of his amusement was nice. His face lit up when he laughed. It made him seem almost human.

"No, not a unicorn. If he had been, the power from stripping his magic from him may have killed me, and we wouldn't converse about it. He's a eunuch."

Flame commanded the servant.

"Show her."

The man opened his robes, showing her his scarred and disfigured, missing masculinity. Hannah sucked in a breath and covered her mouth with one hand as she stared wide-eyed at the man.

When she tore her eyes away, the servant adjusted his robes and stared at the floor, waiting for Hannah to decide his fate.

"Will you keep him?"

Hannah nodded. If she said 'no', she thought Flame would kill him.

Flame was powerful. Crossing him would be a dangerous thing to do. His face hardened when he saw the servant's face.

Flame was angry with the servant. Hannah didn't want Flame angry with her for refusing to accept the gift of a personal servant. Keeping him seemed like the only option.

"You may continue to serve. She finds you tolerable. Prepare the bath for her. She wishes it to be rather hot. Add bubbles."

Hannah's man bowed as he ran off to do as he'd been told.

Flame grumbled something under his breath about how he should have tortured the fool longer for even thinking to touch the treasured things claimed by a dragon while he rummaged through the other wardrobe.

He lightly fingered a spear, then withdrew dress slacks and a shirt. He took out a pair of fine quality black dress shoes and turned to the chest for clean underwear.

Hannah watched him move. His muscles rippled beneath his clothes. Flame moved with grace and fluid movement.

She wondered if he danced. He would be an excellent leading male partner if he did.

She could almost imagine being led onto the floor on his arm and dancing the night away at a masquerade or a ball. It seemed to suit him somehow. He had old-world charm and grace.

When he turned back to face her, she stood transfixed, studying his muscle structure and admiring his athletic appearance.

Hannah got lost in the fantasy of dancing with a handsome man. She shouldn't fantasize about Flame.

What if he had a wife or something? The thought made the night before even worse. She pushed it aside.

"Should I disrobe so you can study me in complete detail?"

He had a silly, lopsided grin.

Hannah almost nodded, then blushed, embarrassed to be so openly admiring Flame's body. What was wrong with her? But she couldn't help herself.

CHAPTER NINE
Uncomfortable

Hannah

"I'm sorry. The way you move... Do you dance?"

She blurted out the question. Then she clapped both hands over her mouth.

She had to get a grip. She couldn't blurt questions at him. He might get offended.

Had she learned nothing in the last couple of weeks? Just because he said he wouldn't hit her didn't mean he wouldn't do it.

"I dance. I like it. It seems we have something besides needing a bath in common. Now, please choose something to wear. I can't allow any of my brothers the singular pleasure of seeing you *sensa vestiti*. It's bad enough you smell divinely of lavender."

Did Flame speak Italian? He liked the way she smelled? He thought seeing her naked was a pleasure?

He was handsome, but maybe he was just flirting with her. She lacked experience with men. Dating had never worked out.

She'd never been interested in a temporary arrangement. Children certainly hadn't figured into her life plan.

The dance was her life. She didn't have time for a hopeless or useless fling. Most men just wanted to sleep with a shapely redhead.

Flame had proved that was exactly what he wanted to do in a way when she bargained for his blood before dawn. He could've had whatever he wanted, and he knew it. She couldn't deny him. He'd only asked to sleep with a redhead.

Did he tease her or flirt with her? She probably wasn't even his type. He'd taken nothing from her. He admitted to liking to dance, but he hadn't offered to dance with her.

Why should she be upset by any of that? Some ridiculous part of her had wanted him to offer. She'd wanted no other man to dance with her.

Hannah had many partners before. Some had even hinted they would like something more than a professional relationship, but she'd always politely declined them. They'd been handsome, too.

Hannah shook her head and put on a robe. Picked out jeans and a blouse, panties, and a bra and almost left the room before she saw herself in the mirror.

Her eyes were black. Not like she landed on the balance bar with her face black eye, but her irises, which used to be a sparkly green, were black.

She touched her face and peered at her reflection. She trembled again, back in shock. What the hell had happened to her eyes?

Flame dropped his clothes on the bed. He had her turned away from the mirror and into his chest as he held her.

"It's okay. I think I know what happened. They used to be green, right?"

Hannah nodded into his chest.

Thankfully, she'd ruined his undershirt at dawn, so she need not worry when her tears streaked some more red on it.

She ruined his clothes, and he continued holding her. The smell of cognac and linen wrapped around her, and he waited for her to regain her calm.

"If they bother you, don't look at them. I need to do some research. Maybe I can fix them or let you have them both ways. I won't leave you like that, okay?"

Flame tried to reassure her as he held her and lightly stroked her hair.

He seemed to know so much. Could he fix her eye color? How? What would it cost her? How did he know?

He called himself a dragon. What did he mean? She would never learn if she didn't ask questions. She took a chance because she needed to understand.

"How did you know about the bathwater?"

Why that question? Who knew?

Hannah had always liked it hot. She'd been born touching the fire. Hot was better.

How long since she'd been really warm? Only with Flame had she managed it in weeks. She missed the flame. She needed her fire.

"That you are *den lasair*? Don't deny it. You were born touching the flame. Only the red-haired, green-eyed women of the O'Keefe sept could do it. You seem sad every time I extinguish my flame. My only real question was, why didn't you bring the flame for yourself?"

"I can't. I mean, I could before, but now..."

Hannah trailed off. She didn't want to remember why. How did he know?

"Come on. Let's get clean, and if you want, I'll listen to your story. It would help to know why you no longer can. That may have something to do with why your eyes are the wrong color."

She was uncertain. She didn't want to remember, but he offered her hope. Maybe the price wouldn't be too high.

Flame seemed to think there was an easy fix, or at least a way for him to change things. She looked at him, but couldn't think of anything to do but go with him to bathe.

It hadn't been an optional statement. Flame didn't notice her reticence. He simply held the door open for her.

She picked up her chosen clothes and walked out of the room. He led her to a large hall bathroom with both a shower and a tub already piled high with bubbles. Hannah wanted to slip into them and soak. She looked at Flame.

He stepped into the shower and turned on the water. Flame stripped off his clothes and threw his ruined undershirt away. His boxers he dropped in the hamper.

He wasn't shy about his nudity in front of her. He stepped into the shower and closed the door. Flame seemed to feel her reticence, and didn't look at her. At least he gave her that small privacy.

Hannah felt guilty for watching him, but he hadn't even questioned her. He'd let her look, knowing she did it.

Was he so sure of himself? Why was he so damn sexy? She waited for him to close his eyes and lather his hair before she took off her clothes.

It was silly. He'd seen her completely naked at least twice already. It still felt uncomfortable.

CHAPTER TEN
Negate The Fact

Hannah

She should want male attention at her age. She was in excellent physical condition, or she had been two weeks ago.

Now her eye color no longer matched who she was. She was no longer what she'd always been.

She left her nightdress in the hamper. Hannah briefly wondered how laundry worked around the place. She'd already admitted she would stay. She could help.

Maybe she'd be less of a burden, less indebted to Flame. If she worked as a maid, perhaps sex wouldn't be the requested method of payment.

She sank into the overly warm water. The bubbles came up to her chin. Hannah sighed her relief. She dipped her head beneath the water and scrubbed her face.

She had a few freckles scattered across her cheeks and her nose. Her aunt had always laughed when she complained about them. 'Character' the old lady had always remarked.

Hannah scrubbed her skin and washed her hair twice before adding conditioner so the curls wouldn't dry in a tangled mess. When the bubbles were almost gone, and the water had cooled, she let the water go and grabbed her towel, quickly wrapping it around herself before she stepped out of the tub. She used a second towel to wrap her hair, so she could brush her teeth and put on lotion.

Flame dressed. He looked sharp in a tailored dress shirt, tailored slacks, and black dress socks. He looked startlingly like a banker or a stockbroker.

Did being a dragon mean he worked in banking or money management?

Flame kept his dark auburn hair neatly trimmed. It was just long enough to touch his shirt collar on the back. He ran a comb through it.

He'd shaved, but kept a small thin mustache and a goatee beard.

Flame leaned against the door frame, watching her dry her hair. It made her self-conscious.

Hannah finished drying her hair and pinned the sides up on top of her head. The rest she let cascade down her back. She didn't bother putting it in her usual bun; it would take longer.

He turned and faced the door when she got ready to dress. Flame didn't offer to leave the room. He waited for her.

When she stepped up next to him, he opened the door, and they walked back to the room they had left. The sheets were all clean. Someone had made the bed.

The scent of freshly cleaned wood floors filled the room. There was no dust. Someone polished the furniture.

"Your servant likes the idea of staying alive."

Flame remarked with dark amusement.

"Hannah's man did this?"

"You should make sure he polishes your silver jewelry once a week, too. What else would you like for him to do? He lives only to serve you."

Hannah didn't have any jewelry, much less silver of any kind.

"But I don't have any silver jewelry."

"Sure you do. It's in the top drawer of the chest on the left. Gold is on the right. Gemstones in the middle. I don't like platinum much, but if you prefer it, I'm sure we can arrange for you to have it as well."

She walked over to the chest and opened the top drawer. It was as he said. Rings, earrings, bracelets, necklaces, pendants, some with gemstones, others without.

She fingered them. They were beautiful. Some were older pieces, but all finely made. There must be thousands of dollars in that drawer alone.

Hannah bent and opened the drawers on the bottom of the wardrobe and found shoes. Dress shoes, sandals, and tennis shoes sat next to heels, boots, and some cute pumps. They were all in her size, just as she had answered him.

Flame never intended to let her go. He said she could leave, but he didn't want her to go anywhere. He'd more than made her comfortable.

Flame had created the perfect gilded cage. She had nice clothes, shoes, and jewelry. She could stay and drink from him every day at dawn. What did he get from it?

Flame got a puppet who couldn't argue with him. She would look pretty, smile, and nod if he took her out somewhere, and she would what? Wait for him to get bored with her and move on to the next conquest?

Hannah wanted to scream. What about her life? What about her dreams, and what she'd worked for in college for the last six years?

She didn't want to be a caged-bird forced to sing her misery. She didn't want the jewelry, shoes, or expensive clothes.

"I don't want any of this. I just want my life back, and I want to dance," she whispered.

None of the fine things mattered to her. She didn't want to stay trapped by her need for the man's blood. She didn't even know his real name.

She sank to her knees before the wardrobe and fingered the pretty sandals. She might as well wear them. It wasn't the shoes' fault her life had fallen apart.

"I know you didn't ask for what happened to you, but I can't change that. What I could alter was your physical comfort at this point. If you don't like the clothes, we can donate them to charity, and I'll take you to purchase items to your liking."

Flame had knelt next to her. He murmured, trying to help her.

"It's not the clothes, or shoes, or the jewelry, or the matching underwear. They're fine, better than anything I've ever owned. It's that none of this is anything like how I envisioned my life. I worked hard to finish school. I auditioned for several positions, and I was so close..."

She trailed off.

"Who are you, Flame? Why do you even care? What does it matter to you what I think?"

She should have curbed her tongue, maybe. She was angry. Hannah had been close to achieving her goals. It was all but lost to her as she was.

Those three other men had destroyed a lifetime's worth of work. Flame wasn't responsible for how she felt, but somehow he was the only one who listened. Why he would care didn't negate the fact he seemed to.

CHAPTER ELEVEN
The Mark

Flame

"My real name is Diarmuid Cinead, and I'm six hundred and twenty-nine years old in this life, although I've died several times. I'm an invincible, immortal shifter, your dragon. What you think matters to me because you are *everything*."

Flame told her the strangest true story. He needed her to believe him. He doubted she would.

She was young. She was both hurt and lost. He had to be patient.

"A dragon what?"

None of it made sense to her. Flame knew she was new to the unseen, immortal world. The Leaindeail still felt strange, even to him.

She seemed to not even know about her magic. He guessed no one bothered to explain it to her. Who turned a woman into a vampire with magic and left her powerless?

It had to be dragons. No vampire would've done that. She was far too powerful for another vampire to have turned her. He needed to understand as much as she did.

"I'm an immortal dragon shifter. I have two forms. In this form, I appear as a man. If I shift, I appear as a grey dragon. My dragon appearance is asleep at the moment, but at sunset today, I will swear allegiance to my king and wake the dragon once again. Do you require proof of my words?"

She nodded.

He looked at her as he smiled a decidedly sharp-toothed grin and smoke curled up from his nostrils. He forced the shift of one hand so she could see his paw with its scales and his razor-sharp claws.

Then he let the flames ignite over his paw. Hannah had thought perhaps he was something like her. He had flames too, but nothing as beautiful or pure as what she had.

He let his paw shift back into his hand. Shifting it was hard while his dragon slept. Only her nearness had let him hold it for so long. Flame left the flames because they seemed to ease her suffering somehow.

She reached out to touch them. He knew she longed to handle them. She was den lasair. He wondered why she didn't call her own. She'd said she couldn't. Why not?

"Will you stay and allow me to help you?"

Hannah nodded her head, resigned to stay. He wished she would smile at him just once. She was so sad. Flame wished he could give her the life she'd worked for back, but he couldn't.

She would have to come to terms with what she was and what her limitations were. It would take time. If he could help her gain something back, she might trust him more.

"You don't seem enthusiastic about staying. Would you rather leave?"

If she wanted to go, he'd take her. He might have to camp out near her for a couple of days until the effects of giving her his blood faded, but he'd do it.

Flame would never recover from the loss if she asked him to leave her, but she mattered more. He'd do as she requested of him. He'd already proven to himself he could deny her nothing.

"You don't want me to leave."

"No, I don't. But I knew that already. What I need to know is what you want to do."

Was she trying to do what he wanted? That made no sense. She was a vjestice vampire. If she commanded him, he would obey. She had magic.

She didn't know. He wondered again, who turned a vjestice vampire and left her defenseless? It was wrong on so many levels he had a hard time wrapping his mind around it.

"I can't leave. Something is wrong with me. They did something to me. I thirst. You don't understand. No one should have a curse such as mine. You offered me the only thing which stops the thirst from destroying me. I made it only four days before it consumed my mind this time, but sometimes I wake with thirst. I don't understand it. There's no hope left. I despair and resent my lost life."

"Who did something to you?"

Flame barely kept the anger out of his voice.

If he found the ones responsible, he'd end them. She was a treasure to him, and destroying the ones who hurt her felt like a responsibility.

She sighed and began her story. He left the idea of leaving alone. If she thought she would stay, he accepted it.

"Two weeks ago, I stayed late at the studio, finishing the paperwork for the director. If I got the call I expected, I would need to leave Houston on good terms because I had high hopes of travelling abroad with a dancing troupe. I walked out to my car, but it had a flat tire. What are the odds?"

She looked at him and shrugged.

"I opened the trunk and took out the tools to change it. When I closed the trunk, a man stood there. He dressed as you do, but shorter and not as powerful. He offered to help me, but I told him I was okay. Turning down an offer for help was the wrong choice."

Hannah shuddered.

"I don't know what happened next. I mean, I only know bits and pieces. The events are fuzzy and warped. I'm not sure they're in the right order. There were three of them. They all looked alike. For a little while, I thought they were all the same man. I have three bite marks, one on my neck and one on the inside of each wrist."

Hannah let him see her wrists.

That there were three bites likely mattered. He studied her wrists. It appeared similar to the pattern followed in sedr magic, which worked on the law of threes. He studied her wrists.

Each bite differed from the others. He let his fingers trail over the marks, soothing away her sadness.

She didn't resist. She seemed to like his touch. That gave him hope.

"May I see the mark on your neck?"

CHAPTER TWELVE

Unintelligible

Flame

Hannah moved her hair away from her left side and pulled the collar of her blouse to one side. The fang marks there didn't resemble either of the other two. He let the fingers of one hand trail down her neck. Her skin was soft and warm.

The mark angered him. It was definitely three different dragon bites. Flame was certain the men who bit her were dragons.

She was only recently turned into a vjestice, just two weeks. Her magic was incredibly strong. It made little sense. Worse, he wanted to bite her, too.

"Did they all bite you at the same time?"

It might matter. It might not. Better to learn all he could. Flame needed to take his mind away from his crazed desire. He had let her drink from him. The magic pressed him to drink from her.

"I don't know. I think so, but the pain was so intense I thought I would die."

Flame didn't bother to tell her she probably had died. It would be nice if she hadn't, but likely as not, she had. Most vampires, turned with magic, died from the bite when they didn't swear. The blood stopped them from entering the Netherworld. The soul returned to the body it knew, but death still occurred.

"What do you remember next?"

"I woke up thirsty. I've never been so thirsty. No matter how much water I drank, it didn't abate. I begged for water."

She paused and wrinkled her nose before continuing.

"A man, who smelled like garlic pickles, handed me a glass. I drank it, but the thirst continued unchanged. I clawed at my throat until the blood ran out. The man laughed at me. I was weak and delirious with a thirst that refused to quench. I panicked. He, He..."

Hannah closed her eyes. She hugged herself.

Flame ached to ease her suffering, but it was in her mind, not her body. He could only wait to see if she would continue. Did she have the strength to tell her story, or would he need to wait?

"He beat me."

She whispered it as if saying it too loudly might cause it to happen again.

Flame hissed in anger. She cringed, but as if compelled, she continued the tale.

He tried to rein in his natural response, so she wouldn't be frightened. He wanted to kill the ones who beat her. That would never happen again.

"He told me I was stupid. When I fell to the floor, he kicked me around the room. When he grew bored, he slit his wrist and held it to my lips. 'This is the only thing that will stop your thirst,' he told me."

"I didn't want it. Who drinks blood? Vampires and crazy people high on flakka, that's who. I tried not to. I didn't want it. He held my nose closed. I had to breathe. It tasted like garlic pickles, it, I … I didn't want it."

Hannah scrunched her pretty face up in anger. Her tiny hands balled into fists. They turned her without consent. Had she been a shifter, she would be dead already.

As it was, she slowly faded. She didn't wish to live as a vampire. Flame needed to stop the fade from happening, but how?

The man had overpowered her and turned her with too much dragon blood. Three drops were all he should've given her. Only other vampires gave away so much blood. Their blood wasn't as strong with the veritas magic as dragon blood. They had to give more to turn another into a vampire.

Flame put his arm around her shoulders. He wanted to give her his strength and support. He also desperately needed to feel her body close to his. She leaned against him and breathed. When she calmed down, Hannah continued the story.

"The room spun. I passed out. The next time I woke up, I burned with a fever. A different man found me awake. He looked the same, but he smelled worse, like sauerkraut and onions. He asked me what I needed. I turned my face away from him. He grabbed me by the hair and jerked my head back so hard I thought my neck snapped. My mouth flew open to scream, but I drowned in the blood instead."

"'Next time answer properly,' he told me before he dropped me to the floor. I couldn't move. I couldn't feel my body. My mouth betrayed my mind and swallowed every drop, and my tongue licked my face clean."

Flame had to interrupt her. He wanted to smash things and kill something a few times, but he needed information. He had to remain in control.

She already feared him. He had no intention of making it worse. Punching holes in the walls might relieve some of his aggravation, but it would only frighten her more, so he held his anger in check.

"Did he feed it to you from his vein or pour it into your mouth?"

Hannah blinked. Flame had brought her out of her story. She concentrated hard, thinking. He admired the way her scrunched brow looked. Hannah was gorgeous.

"From his wrist. He cut it longways so it would pour out quickly, and he could leave me faster, I think."

Hannah nodded as if she agreed with her own words.

"What happened next?"

She studied him for only a second before she launched back into the story. Had she wanted to say something else? Why did she cut herself off like that?

He had to watch the behavior. It wasn't good. He saw her as a clear submissive, and she feared his size and power. Something else crossed her face.

Was she forced to comply with his wishes? How could that be? She was a vjestice vampire. She should give orders, not receive them.

"I don't remember if I slept. I think I must have, but I don't remember."

Hannah had died again. They'd killed her twice, for sure. Chances were good she would die one more time. Why kill her three times, though?

"I shivered uncontrollably. My teeth wouldn't stop chattering. I am den lasair. I have never been cold before. It was disconcerting. The third man, who looked the same but smelled like rotten eggs, found me rolled into a ball, shivering violently. He asked me what I needed. My teeth chattered so violently I couldn't say it. I tried, but even I knew it was unintelligible."

CHAPTER THIRTEEN
Turn Away

Flame

She raised her hands to shield her head.

"I tried to protect my head. It was no use. He told me when I woke up, I would never defy another command again. His foot connected with my ear and things went black."

Hannah shivered. Flame allowed the fire to ignite and warmed her. He eased her into his lap and held her close to his chest. His heart hurt.

She didn't understand, but what they had done to her was probably irreversible. They'd made her a broken vjestice.

Only dragon blood would calm the thirst. They'd deliberately given her too much and required her to request it, even though she neither wanted it nor was she offered a proper chance to answer.

Thankfully, it had been three of them, or he'd have had no chance to save her from her thirst.

Hannah couldn't give orders. As a vjestice vampire, she had magic. She should be able to levitate, create fire and ice, use allure, and command the servants with nothing more than a thought.

She could only follow orders after what they did to her. They'd killed her three times dealing with commands. She'd always be submissive.

He'd have to protect her. Other dragons could harm her if they ordered her or even made a strong suggestion. Strong shifters or even other vampires might cause her an issue. He didn't even want to think about humans.

If he sealed her to himself, he could severely lessen the effect. If she accepted him as her consort, she would submit to him as her alpha. She would want to please her mate.

She'd inherently avoid other men and follow his directives, anyway. He just had to be careful not to influence her responses. That was a lot of 'ifs'. How the hell was he supposed to manage all of that?

None of it explained why her eyes were black. He needed to know the rest, but hunger gnawed at his stomach. He took out his phone and texted the servant to bring him two food trays and some beef jerky. Using so much of his magic to help Hannah was creating a need for far more calories.

"Flame, are you okay?"

She was the one who'd been born with part of her magic missing, and she asked him if he was okay? It was too much. He would have to explain it to her, eventually.

Flame breathed and remained calm. He didn't want to cause her more anxiety.

"I'm struggling, Nightshade. Honestly, I wish to hunt these three and murder them. The dragon in me sees you as a great treasure. I desire to hoard you for myself. That another harmed my claimed treasure angers me greatly. I need to take care of you more than I wish to do violence. I have control. Have no fear. You're safe with me. You've done nothing wrong. Those who hurt you are the ones I'm angry at."

Flame wanted to reassure her.

"I confess I fear your strength, but oddly, I feel safe with you."

Flame had ordered her to have no fear. She couldn't comply with his request. She confessed her inability, fearing his anger. Things would be tough.

He wished he had his and Blaze's sedr magic scrolls. He wanted to read more, but Flame understood her inability to calm the thirst and her inability to order a servant with her will rather than her words.

Flame nodded at her words, accepting them. She calmed. He could build trust if he remained in control of himself.

The servant arrived with his dinner, and Flame helped Hannah to her feet. He offered Hannah tea. She looked at it oddly, unsure of it. She knew nothing of what she was.

"Nightshade, you're a vjestice vampire. Dragons turned you, using veritas magic. It's the magic of blood. You have magic available to you. I can teach you if you like. You can drink tea, soda, juice, coffee, water, and alcohol. Avoid milk. Would you like some tea?"

Flame was careful to phrase his requests, so she had the option to choose.

Hannah nodded, and he served her a glass of iced tea. They clinked their glasses together, smiling a little, and he attacked the food.

She drank her tea and sighed at her small pleasure. He knew she felt good to have a taste of her life back. When one could have nothing else, tea was a luxury.

"I would like you to teach me, please. I miss touching the flame."

He would teach her. He'd do anything to help her. Whatever she requested of him, Flame would do.

"Nightshade, I have to go out at sunset. I have some business to settle. Will you be all right here?"

Hannah cowered a little. His blood called to him to bite her and taste her as she'd tasted him. Blood started the bond between lifemates. Not staying with her would be torture.

He needed to stay near her, to claim her, but to be a dragon, he had to leave her and swear his oath. Not going would lead to inquiries he couldn't face.

He wanted to serve. Luke was the Dire Wolf King. He had hope after centuries of none.

"The servants will be here. Your servant can guard the door if you like. I have a cell phone for you. It's pre-programmed with the numbers of the dragons and the Council members. Someone warded the house against evil. You're safe here."

Flame wished to allay her fears.

Flame rose and took the cell phone she had used earlier from the top of the chest and handed it to her when she nodded her acceptance of the situation. Taking her with him wasn't an option. She would distract him.

The oath swearing would be difficult. He almost sighed, but thought better of it. Flame didn't want to leave her.

"I should return before midnight. I wish to hear the rest of your story. You may tell me the rest when I return."

He realized too late, he'd worded his request too strongly. She'd fulfill his desire to hear her story.

Well, it would keep her safe. He needed to help her so he could claim her. His hand cupped her face, and he sighed as he forced himself to turn away from her.

CHAPTER FOURTEEN

An Investment

Flame

He rode to the ceremony with Blaze. No one bothered him about his unusual quietness. They probably assumed his reserve was respect for Blaze.

Blaze had bled for Grace when she died. His blood called to him.

Leaving Grace to go to the ceremony pulled him apart. It had been life or death. Blaze was guilty of no crime. His old friend simply hurt. Silence allowed him to concentrate.

Flame was closer to Blaze than any of his brothers. Blaze had helped him make it through the worst times. If anyone would understand what Flame had done, it would be Blaze. Flame still didn't speak.

He preferred to battle the aching need to return to Hannah alone. The last thing he needed was to turn his closest friend into an accomplice to his wrongdoing. Blaze couldn't suffer for Flame's choices.

He feared his other brothers wouldn't understand. Ash, least of all.

Blaze alone knew the truth of Flame's past, and he'd kept his promise not to speak of it for over five hundred years. It remained complicated.

Flame was unsure he could face it again. Better to leave it in the past and face the future.

He made it through the ceremony. He'd done it countless times for different kings over the years. It was a matter of routine.

Flame had chosen it this time, but he was still not fully comfortable with his decision. He wanted to serve, but his heart was with Hannah.

Shifting into his dragon felt good. It eased the stress and pressure. The animal mind accepted things as they were without the complication of the human layers.

Being a dragon was a relief. Letting the flames go after so long, let the stress burn away.

He stretched his wings. He felt like his wings remained furled in a tight, dusty room for too many centuries. Minus the dusty room. His wings had been furled for too long.

Three hundred years he'd walked the earth as only a man. Finally, his dragon slept no more.

After wandering the forest as a dragon for a while, letting all of his anxieties fade away, Flame followed his brothers back to the little cabin to wait for the pack. Fox and Artie were there.

Flame tried to take part in the conversation for a bit, but his thoughts had returned to Hannah. When he spoke, it was about her. What if she didn't want a consort?

Hannah was a vampire. She didn't have to take a mate. She was beautiful, but broken. If she left Draoithe, it would be easy for a strong male to take advantage of her.

He had to find a way to at least keep her at Draoithe for her safety. All the time he'd spent studying magic and vampires, and he still didn't know enough.

The ride back was uneventful. Flame put his hand on Blaze's shoulder. He knew his brother was anxious for Grace.

He'd joked and tried to join the conversation earlier, but his mind had been with Grace. No one else would know. He was as stoic as always, but Flame could see the signs in the ticking of his jaw muscles.

The two dragons had worked too close for far too many years for Flame not to read him. Blaze nodded. Their friendship had long since passed the need for words.

Blaze was so serious and straight-laced. Being the dungeon master for the kingdom of Leinster had made him taciturn. Why, out of all the dragons, he and Blaze were so tight, was beyond Flame.

Flame had been the playboy of the group. Blaze was more the strong, silent type. Char was succinct to near bluntness. Smoke was amiable, nosy. Lightning was quick-witted, Ember was slow to decide. Ash was the lone leader.

He knew them all well, but it was Blaze who'd been his stalwart friend throughout the centuries.

They arrived back at the dragon's house, and his brothers all scattered back to their current missions. They had orders to care for their Valkyries. It was their sole responsibility. Hannah was all he could focus on, anyway.

Being back in her presence eased the pull on his magic. He could tolerate it as long as he could see her and smell the lavender.

Soon he would feel her bite him again. His desire rose, but he tamped it back down. It was not the right time. It could wait until dawn when it was safe.

He didn't want a thrall. He wanted his mate.

Seeing Hannah's black eyes looking up at him expectantly pulled at his heart. How could he tell her how broken she was? How they made her wrong as a vjestice? Was there a way to correct what happened to her?

He needed his scrolls. Flame longed to discuss the situation with Blaze, but it was the wrong time. Blaze had enough problems. Flame needed to work it out himself.

He needed the rest of her story to help her. She was likely only still there because he'd approached, commanding her to stay with the way he'd worded his earlier request.

She also knew he'd allow her to drink from him at dawn. It had to get better. He wanted her to desire to stay, to desire him as he desired her.

"Flame, you seem agitated. Did your meeting not go well?"

Hannah asked with what appeared to be a genuine concern.

Why should she care about his meeting? He wanted her to care, but he couldn't delude himself with how she'd done anything more than make idle conversation to kill the silence which stretched between them.

"It went well. I swore fealty to my king. He accepted my oath. The dragon no longer sleeps."

"I'm sorry. You speak in riddles. Who is this king?"

Hannah truly knew nothing.

"Luke Mendez is the Dire Wolf King. The one giving orders when I rescued you. He's a direwolf shifter they raised as the Ri ruirech, the overlord of Draoithe. It's him whom I serve. My oath finished my shifter magic. I can shift fully into my dragon form."

"Draoithe is a kingdom?"

"Sort of. You've entered the immortal world, the Leaindeail. We're part of the rest of the dream."

Flame smiled at the cute, confused face she presented with her wrinkled forehead and pursed lips when he did a terrible job explaining things.

"We're technically outside of Tyler, TX. But humans don't really know we exist. We always appear as people to them. It can be dangerous living among humans. We hide, and our laws and customs govern our society."

She nodded.

"If you'll allow me, I'll teach you while you're here. While this house is a temporary home for the dragons, Luke's constructing a retreat for immortals. It's nearly finished. We should move to a new location soon."

"We?"

Nightshade had yet to meet the other denizens of Draoithe.

"The Druid pack, the dragons, and all the sanctuary guests and dragonsworn servants."

"Is it as nice as this house?"

"Much nicer. If you choose to stay, I think you'd like it. Tell me. What did you do while I was gone?"

She sat in the middle of the floor in workout clothes. She had put her hair up.

"I practiced while I thought about things. I think better when I move."

He wanted to see her move. His cock wanted in on the idea.

"Do you tango?"

She looked up at him and nodded slowly.

"Would you accompany me? What music would you prefer?"

"You wish to dance with me?"

Her question held a breathy quality, excited, but suddenly shy.

"If you would."

He left it open.

She jumped up and set the music on the phone. It was a traditional orchestra. He took up the proper pose in front of her. For the first time, she truly smiled at him. His soul sang.

He'd always loved the party, the dance, the music, and the atmosphere. One of the few memories he had from his life before he became a dragon was dancing with a beautiful red-haired woman.

Hannah joined him. They stepped to the downbeat, and she let him lead. They stepped around the tight, open space of the room.

She smiled a genuine smile for him the entire time, always looking away. Ahh, the tango. He could watch her without her seeing him watch her.

Dancing with her was an erotic and powerful expression of grace. She floated through the steps like liquid grace.

As the song neared its end, he put her through the last turn. She was in his arms, and he dipped her back for the finish.

When they got up, it was over. She looked into his eyes. His arms encircled her back.

His desire to kiss her clear on his face, she lifted on tiptoe and kissed him so lightly her lips barely touched his.

He drew her closer and pressed his lips to hers. He let it linger, light and divine, for a long moment. Then he released her and stepped back.

Pressing her would be wrong. If she never kissed him again, he would know one had been real. It may be the only kiss he would ever truly remember.

"You're the best partner I've ever had the pleasure of dancing with. We should go out and embarrass people sometime."

He ginned.

"You may have missed your calling. That was fantastic! I would love to go dancing with you."

She agreed to go on a date with him. She felt as if he asked her out. It was a game he knew well. It was the one game he could play, and it was for keeps.

"When is it good for you? I'm available all this week. Name the night, and I'll learn where to go."

He let her choose when.

"How about Friday? I know a place in Dallas with only a small crowd."

Her enthusiasm gave him hope.

"Friday it is. Can you be ready by half-past sundown?"

She nodded, smiling a beautiful, perfect smile. He grinned back at her.

"Nightshade, would you have a drink with me?"

Flame wanted to share the night with her. He wanted to breathe lavender, drink cognac, and suffer the enchantment of a beautiful vampire.

If there was one thing he'd enjoyed while he worked for the enclave in Romania, it was the parties they threw. Vampire women were beautiful.

"Yes."

"What would you care to drink?"

"I don't know. I never drink."

"Would you like to try some wine?"

She nodded.

He grinned and opened the door for her. When he stepped into the hallway, she took his arm. He was an old school gallant and oh, so charming. He felt she needed the polite etiquette. They made their way to the bar in the living room.

After one in the morning, no one would bother them. He stepped to the bar and served two drinks. She sat on the sofa. He handed her a glass of wine.

"Sip it. It will be slightly bitter at first, but as you go, it tastes sweeter."

He joined her on the couch.

She tried it and made a face. He laughed. She smiled. They talked.

She asked him what he did, and he explained about being an investment specialist, but avoided boring her with numbers.

CHAPTER FIFTEEN
The Room Spun

*H*annah

He drank his cognac and enjoyed her company. He was charming and handsome. The potent wine made her light-headed.

Flame made her forget for a minute all the things which weighed on her mind. Dancing with him had been divine. Flame had enjoyed himself.

Hannah could see he'd wanted to kiss her, but he was too much of a gentleman to force her. He let her choose. She kissed him.

Thrilling and dangerous, for the first time, she enjoyed it. It felt right, as if she should kiss him without the dance routine. She might like to do it again sometime. Denying her attraction to Flame was a waste of time.

Hannah studied his face. It was masculine, rough, but sexy. She would never have said yes to a date with him before, but it felt good to talk with him. She liked his voice, the kindness in his eyes, and the charm he displayed for her. It was a sublime, surreal moment in the aftermath of a tragic episode.

"A penny for your thoughts?"

His query came with a charming smile when she grew quiet.

"I wondered how you do it?"

"How do I do what?"

Flame frowned.

"How do you steal my focus and put it on you?"

She had to know.

She'd felt no attraction so strongly before. He stole her breath and became like a single-minded obsession. Considering what happened, it seemed peculiar.

"Shifters have one person in the dream who can be their lifemate. If we're lucky enough or search long and hard enough, we may find them. I found her. She is you."

He grinned a shy smile, telling her he knew she would never believe him.

"The shifter magic is what you feel. I wish to make my mate happy, so it complies with my desire. When you have anxiety, the magic will leech your fear away. If you become overly stressed, it will attempt to calm you. It will only work for you."

She frowned at him. He sighed.

"I'm not doing anything. Because I just wish to ease your distress. My magic encircles you. I feel it happening. It has never happened before. I'm not sure how it works, exactly. It feels… right."

"Flame, it can't be me. It would never work."

She had to explain. Things happened to her, and he deserved better than what he'd ever get with her. There was no way things would stay good, and she feared his anger if he believed she misled him. She wouldn't have measured up, even without the trauma, but there was no hope.

"Would you mind explaining?"

He sat still, listening.

"I could never give you what you deserve. They did things to me, I can't…"

Hannah looked away from him.

"Nightshade, you kissed me. Forgive me if I've made a mistake here, but I thought you wanted to kiss me. Was I wrong?"

Flame searched her face for the truth he needed to see. She had kissed him, not the other way around. He didn't press her. He'd only made his desire plain.

"No, I wanted to kiss you. Dancing with you was amazing. I wanted to kiss you again, but I'm afraid. Flame, I have little experience. When they took me, I had never..."

Hannah trailed off. She never imagined having *that* conversation with a man before. She couldn't explain. Was it why people didn't drink?

She looked at her glass. It was nearly empty. The room felt tilted. Was one glass enough to make someone drunk?

What did being drunk feel like? Maybe tilted rooms were part of it.

Hannah looked back at Flame. He stared at her, thinking hard. He looked good in concentration.

She wanted to reach out and touch him, but her fear kept her hands from his face.

He was like a beautiful piece of art she wanted to own so she could admire it at her leisure forever and never share it with anyone else. It couldn't be. There was so much she just didn't understand.

"Nightshade, tell me what they did to you."

Flame commanded her. Like a dutiful servant, she obeyed.

"For days after I had awoken freezing, they took turns abusing me. One right after the other. The first time, they beat me until I called the flame. I only wanted the pain to stop. As soon as I called the flame to me, they laughed at me. Two of them held me down, while the other broke my teeth. He was chanting over me, then forced his blood into my mouth. After he did, I choked. He forced my mouth closed and made me swallow. They switched places and repeated the process, and then again. Afterward, I could no longer touch the flame. They beat me afterward. I reached for the flame, but it would no longer come to me."

"What were the words they used? Tell them to me."

Flame ordered her to speak the words. She had to concentrate hard, unsure of the words. Her head spun. She'd drunk too much wine.

"To block the fire, stop the sire. Steal the flame until the name."

"Did each one repeat the phrase three times?"

"Yes."

"They sealed you, didn't they? They couldn't take your fire, but they sealed you from men. It's why..."

He trailed off as he looked at her. Flame drew his brows together, jumped up, and paced the floor.

Flame looked back at her. Did she look as miserable as she felt? He would not want her. All the stuff he'd said about lifemates couldn't be true.

He just wanted her to be comfortable with him. He probably wanted to enjoy his Saturday night. Instead, he was stuck babysitting a reluctant vampire.

Her thoughts hurt. Perhaps her attraction to him was more than his for her. Polite declination of men's invitations was more her style.

"Tell me the truth, Nightshade. Did you truly want to kiss me?"

"Yes."

She whispered the answer. There was no option not to answer. She had to tell him. The truth was all there was.

"Would you do it again?"

Hannah cringed. Would he force her? She didn't want it. Hannah liked him. But there'd been so much pain and torture. She cringed in fear before him.

"Yes."

She enjoyed kissing him. It made her feel as if she were the most beautiful woman in the world. She liked the attention.

There was something wrong with her. It must be some kind of weird Stockholm syndrome.

"Are you afraid of me?"

She shrank away from him even further. She feared him so much if she could fade into the wall, she would do it to get away from his overbearing aura. He was so alpha, so powerful. Hannah shrank away, petrified with fear.

"Yes."

Would he strike her? He had told her not to be afraid, but she was. She couldn't comply with his demand. She trembled.

"If I demanded it, would you beg me to kiss you?"

"Yes."

She mouthed the word with no sound.

If he demanded it of her, she knew she would do whatever he asked. She seemed to have no option. Why? The cruelty seemed never-ending.

"Beg me then. Beg an alpha male to kiss you as you deserve. Do you want me to kiss you breathless?"

Hannah nodded. She wanted him to kiss her again, even if she knew it was wrong. Even if it would be as it was with the nameless ones, she still wanted it.

"Beg me for it, Nightshade. Beg me as if you want it from only me."

Hannah fell on her face at his feet. She groveled on her knees before him.

"Please, Flame. Kiss me, I need to be kissed breathless. You are the only one who can give me what I need. Please, I need to kiss you. I want to feel your lips pressed against..."

Flame's lips met hers hard as he pulled her roughly up against his body, demanding her full attention. She couldn't breathe. She burned for air, but she couldn't stop.

Her hands slipped around his neck. She didn't wish to let him go. She could feel his desire for her pressed against her. If it was all she could have, she wanted it desperately.

Her lips moved over his lips with passion and determination. He was supposed to kiss her, but now she kissed him. Hannah would kiss him until she couldn't.

She could smell lavender mixed with cognac and linen. Her chest tightened. The edges of her vision went black. The room spun around when she finally fell.

CHAPTER SIXTEEN

Dancing

*F*lame

Flame caught her as she fainted. He lowered her body to the couch and followed her down. The magic pulled him to act. He cut his tongue on his fang.

He spoke her true name in a whisper and kissed her lips with his blood on his lips. He did it nine times in a row. She was his lifemate, the claimed treasure of a dragon. No one would stop him from claiming his mate as his Valkyrie.

He would be lying if he denied enjoying the feel of her in his arms as he kissed her. Taking advantage of an unconscious and drunken vampire wasn't his usual style, but in her case, it was worth it.

Her warmth and weight next to his body excited him in a way he'd almost forgotten he could feel. She made him feel alive in a way he hadn't felt in at least five hundred years.

His kiss wouldn't fix her eyes by itself, but he broke the seal on her. They had sealed her to block her flame. Because she was an O'Keefe woman, she should touch it.

If denied her feminine ability, she couldn't call the fire to her. Flame was the sire. He was the alpha male she would submit to. Flame knew her name. He knew who she was as a Valkyrie. He could give her back her flame.

When she was ready, he would reseal her, but to himself. Her eyes would be green when she appeared human. He could give her back her original appearance if he bonded with her.

They would only be black in her Valkyrie form. His blood would protect her. He could fix that at the least. The rest would take time. He had hope, and he could give her some, too.

If he was right, she'd never been with a man. She said she had no experience. He had to be careful with her. When she said she wanted it, he would take her honor for himself.

She was a vampire. Her vampiric nature intensified her sexuality. There would be immense pain involved. There would be blood. He would be physically bound to her desire ever after.

She alone could destroy him. If she walked away, after that, she may as well run him through with his spear, because he wouldn't recover from that sort of loss again, not if he lost her.

There was absolutely no way he would give up the den lasair vampire. Not when he knew she wanted him as badly as he wanted her. She was fragile.

If he pushed her too hard, she would run from him. He would likely never get another better chance than the one he had at that moment.

He'd commanded her to beg him to kiss her, and she'd turned it around and begged to kiss him. She'd kissed him so fiercely he was the one who wound up breathless.

If she hadn't passed out, he might have died from lack of oxygen. She'd been desperate for him to kiss her.

Too much wine too fast had led to her current unconscious state. The natural faster vampire metabolism would have her conscious again shortly.

Flame sipped his cognac again as he watched her breathe. She was so incredibly beautiful. The magic of the dream had crafted her for him, and she was everything he could've dreamed up.

He reached out his hand and brushed her hair away from her face. Her freckles spellbound flame. He wanted to trace the outline across her cheeks and the bridge of her nose. He was so lost to her.

If she knew the power she had over him, she could wreck his world. He was already in too deep. His fingers caressed her skin and felt the soft silkiness as he breathed her scent.

Flame waited for her to regain herself. It took longer than he thought it would. When she blinked up at him, he sat up to give her room to sit up as well.

"I'm sorry, Nightshade. I should've warned you to drink the wine slower, and I didn't realize you drank it so fast. Are you okay?"

"I think so."

She licked her lips and froze. She could taste his blood on her lips. Hannah scrambled away from him in a panic.

"Did I bite you? I'm sorry. I didn't mean to..."

She thought she'd bitten him? He almost laughed.

"You didn't bite me. Relax. I'm unharmed. I'm worried about you. You passed out. Are you okay?"

She nodded.

"Why do my lips taste like cognac and linen? Like you?"

Cognac and linen? Was that how he tasted? Was that a good or bad flavor? He hoped she thought it was delicious. The dragon inside rose and desired fiercely to bite her. He changed the subject to distract himself.

"Forgive me, but I figured out part of the riddle of your eye color. It's sadly still black, but I know how to correct the problem and give you back your green ones. I fixed your issue with your fire, though. I think you won't mind the taste of cognac and linen if it banishes the cold."

He smiled at her. She blinked.

Then she smiled widely as the flames danced over her palm. Beautiful, pure red flames flickered in her open hand. True happiness and wonder spread over her face. She swirled fire the color of her hair over her fingers and let it pass from one hand to another, entranced with the fire and her ability to feel it again.

She was purely magnificent in her happiness. He wanted to see her always smiling. Flame memorized how she looked. He would never forget it.

Hannah looked back at him.

"Thank you, Flame."

"Trust me, it was my pleasure. Seeing you happy was worth the expenditure of magic, but truthfully, I'm starving. Will you join me for dinner? I'm sure there's tea, or if you prefer, there's blood as well."

Hannah nodded. He offered her his hand to help her rise to her feet, and he led her to the kitchen. He offered her a glass of blood. She tasted it and grimaced. He laughed and served her a glass of tea instead.

Although any blood would keep her alive, only dragon blood would ever stop her thirst. She wasn't a thrall and didn't have blood lust, but she'd overdosed on the dragon blood at her making.

Her vjestice magic was exceptionally powerful. She said they broke her teeth, but she had them all. Hannah stored sedr energy and regenerated. She would be more powerful when she took her consort. Please let him be worthy of her.

Flame rummaged through the refrigerator and pulled out several deli sandwich portions of meat and cheeses. He began stacking the meat on the bread with cheese haphazardly. Hannah watched him and started laughing.

"What's so funny?"

Her laughter and amusement made him smile. He wanted to keep her laughter for himself alone. It was as gorgeous as she was. The dragon's possessive need to hoard its treasure rose in him fiercely, but he kept it in check.

"Your sandwiches. They don't even look like sandwiches. Here, let me do it. How can you even get your mouth around it that way? Do you like mayo or mustard?"

She took his plate and reordered the meats and cheeses.

"Mayo."

She tried to open the jar, but the lid was too tight. He took it from her, opened it, and handed it back to her. She spread the mayo on both slices of bread as she flipped all the sandwiches and sliced them in half. She handed him the plate back with four oversized sandwiches all stacked to the same height and neatly sliced in half.

The presentation was better, although he would have eaten it just the same the other way. Shifters needed food, and dragons needed meat.

He could smell the scent of lavender on his food from her touch. Somehow, she even made ordinary sandwiches better.

"This way you can be as charming while you eat as you were when you danced the tango."

He grinned at her. She thought he was charming. She loosened up; her fear faded. Flame had accomplished something worthwhile, at least. He wanted her to relax and be comfortable with him.

"Friday. I'll talk to Ryker and ensure we have a vehicle. I must take you dancing."

CHAPTER SEVENTEEN

More Powerful

Flame

"Flame, why are you so nice to me? I know you told me about the lifemate thing, but I..."

Hannah trailed off.

"You feel as if I'm feeding you a line so I can get something from you. I know. It sounds crazy. You aren't a shifter, so you don't feel it as I do. It's even worse for me because you have my blood, and it calls me to claim you. Resisting is difficult. You want some proof. There is proof available, but it's sexual, and it starts the bonding process. It would be permanent. Unless you were certain you wanted me, I don't think we should do it."

"Nightshade, you're beautiful. I enjoy your company. I like how you laugh, and the way you dance speaks to me. You're immortal. You have all the time in the dream to see if you and I might be compatible. There's no pressure. I won't pretend I'd easily share your attention with another, but you're a vampire. Most vampires don't take a consort, they usually have many lovers and live in enclaves ruled by women."

"No! No way! I wouldn't know what to do with one man, much less a lot of different ones, because I was never any good at men. I might be the only lone vampire, but I'm okay with that."

Hannah seemed in opposition to the idea of having multiple lovers. Flame wasn't upset by that. He didn't wish for her to have any but himself, but he couldn't tell her.

Besides, none of the men at Draoithe would even look at her for too long, much less think to touch her. It would be obvious to all the shifters she was his, and all the male vampires at Draoithe weren't interested because they had shifter consorts with whom they had bonded.

Would she want more experience? Could he step aside and wait for her? He knew if she asked him, he'd do it.

It would devastate him, and when she grew tired of her lovers, they might not survive. But she was a vampire.

"Flame, you said I have magic, and you could teach me how to use it. What kind of magic? Is it dangerous?"

Hannah's curiosity overrode her anxiety.

The lingering effects of the alcohol faded. Flame finished the last sandwich and left the plate in the sink. Thankfully, she distracted him from his dark murderous thoughts about others she might let touch her.

"All magic is dangerous. You're acquainted with it, so you have some understanding, even if you don't realize it. Shall we walk outside? The house is a bit confining for magic practice."

Hannah walked with him. He grabbed the tea pitcher and a glass. They stepped through the sliding glass doors onto the back porch. Flame listened to the creek at the back of the property. The water gurgled along the rocks. The stars were cool at four in the morning. It was peaceful.

"Let's sit in the gazebo. The creek will help, and if we make any noise, we won't disturb anyone."

"That gazebo belongs to that other house."

She sounded confused, but obediently walked toward the gazebo.

He'd made an order again. He wanted to kick himself.

"All three houses belong to Draoithe."

He pointed out the houses on either side of them.

"They're all occupied by members of the Druid pack. We won't be trespassing. We may not be alone, but we'll be safe."

"Who besides us are even awake?"

"Three other vampires live here, along with a black panther and an owl. The eagle is an insomniac as well. Sometimes, people have nightmares or can't sleep. We try to be respectful."

"They're like me? How many people are there?"

"Nearly fifty if you count the dragonsworn and the sanctuary guests."

"That many? How do they afford all this?"

Hannah had little understanding of how wealth grew.

"Many of the original pack members invested heavily into Draoithe, and the dragons also contributed the Ruiri's shares of our hoards. Draoithe is a multi-billion dollar startup. Money is not an issue."

She readily accepted his explanation, although he didn't think she could truly understand. It was too much money for most people to grasp, so he left it.

They arrived at the gazebo and sat down on a bench. Hannah looked at him expectantly.

"I think you need a bit of a history lesson first. It might frame things better."

She nodded.

"Magic is all controlled with the power of your mind. It deals with thoughts, images, sounds, scents, and memories. All magic requires energy. Sorceresses use light magic from the Ainglean, the realm inhabited by angels and white dragons. Elementals draw the spirit power of distinct elements in the Leaindeail, our realm. Wizards can master it all given enough time. Shifters burn calories to shift, so they have to eat a lot. Druids and necromancers pull dark magic from the Netherworld. Veritas magic uses the power of blood. Sedr magic uses sexual energy to function. Vampire magic, Volos magic, is a combination of the shifter, Druid, and sedr magic. Most vampires have only a small amount. They have enough to make them immortal and use their allure."

"Wait. I'm immortal? Will I live forever? I can't die?"

She hadn't understood that part. Her thoughts reflected those of a human woman.

"Others could kill you, but you will never experience illness or grow old like mortals. Some immortals grow tired of life, especially if they're alone and choose to fade, or with a vampire, they simply meet the dawn."

Hannah became a vampire with little knowledge about what it meant. Being immortal was only beginning to sink in. It would take time, but she was an intelligent woman.

Hannah would be a powerful vjestice. Flame smiled and poured the tea into the glass. He set it on the railing. Hands-on seemed like the best training possible.

"Look at the tea in the glass. I need you to think cold thoughts at the glass. Think about what cold feels like, what it smells like, and what it looks like to you. I want you to concentrate those ideas into one word and project it on the glass with your mind."

Hannah studied the glass for a moment, then the tea froze and the glass frosted over. The air around the glass began to freeze and frost formed on the railing beneath the glass.

"Okay, that's enough."

Flame studied the glass. Most made ice cubes. Hannah started a miniature freezer. She was far beyond the ability most vampires could ever dream of having.

"That was neat!"

Hannah said excitedly.

"That was unbelievable. Now, I need you to call the flame and melt the glass, but don't set fire to the railing. Just think 'heat' at the glass, okay? Don't throw fire at it."

Flame was careful with the fire. She was den lasair. Her fire was already powerful before she became vjestice. It would be much stronger as a vjestice princess.

Hannah concentrated. The tea melted, and all the frost faded. The tea boiled, and Flame asked her to stop. Hannah clapped her hands. Flame grinned at her.

"Stand up."

Hannah jumped to her feet. Flame almost cringed. He had to remember not to command her.

"Concentrate on floating. Try to float straight up in the air until we see eye to eye. I'll steady you. Are you ready?"

He gripped her hands.

She nodded. Flame nodded back.

Hannah lifted about six inches before she got over-excited, lost her balance, and he caught her. Levitation was hard, but she could float up six inches on her first try. That wasn't bad.

"Do you want to try again?"

She nodded and immediately grasped his hands to levitate again. She concentrated on her balance and floated at the same time. Being a dancer was a plus for her levitation.

She rose above him until he was reaching up to hold her hands. Her head bumped the low rafter, and she fell right into his arms. He caught her and spun around with her. They both laughed when he set her on her feet.

"So there are benefits to this dark curse."

"Some call vampirism the dark gift. It has drawbacks, but it has rewards as well. You avoid the sun, but you're made the most beautiful version you could be. It stays forever, and all men desire the vampire. Some people seek vampires for the euphoria associated with their bite. You can have any male you desire with the power of your allure. You'd be a super predator, never aging or losing your faculties. But you can't eat food, so you'll have to drink the life force of another to survive. The more magic you use, the more energy you'll need. But most vampires increase in power as they age.

The stronger your mind, the more powerful you become."

CHAPTER EIGHTEEN

Collected His Thoughts

*F*lame

"The dark gift? It's not all a curse."

Hannah needed to let the thought roll around in her mind a bit. So far in her journey as a vampire, she'd received little good. She needed to see her situation as positive instead of negative.

"Dragons turned you into a vampire with magic. You're rare. To the vampire communities, you are royalty."

He reached out and placed a loose strand of her hair behind her ear. The desire to touch her again overtook him. He couldn't resist.

Mortal men weren't the only ones attracted to vampires. Flame, of all the grey dragons, had a singular infatuation with vampires. With this one in particular.

"You'd be a princess. Only those turned with magic can levitate, move faster than a speeding car, and control ice and fire. In eastern Europe, the vjestice were seers, witches, and women who worshiped the forest god Volos. In return for their loyalty, they received magic. Vampire women were frequently mistaken for them."

"The dragons there were the first to turn men and women with magic. Some of them worked among mortals, so the legends spread. More accurately, the men were the *zduhaci or dragon men*. If a vampire chooses a lover for life, they become consorts. They're bound to each other by magic. If they renounce all other lovers, they can seal themselves to their consort using the sedr and veritas magics. They can never have another, but no other can violate them, either."

"Eventually, the ancient vampires learned to make others like themselves and rose against the dragons who created them. The dragons recruited the phoenixes to help break the revolt. They burned Dracula's castle. The vampires who survived the massacre fled, reforming their society in small groups around the vjestice leaders, and with the help of the basilisks, the vampires murdered all the zduhaci unbound as perpetrators of the massacre."

"Is that why you like me? Is it because I'm this vjestice vampire?"

Hannah desired an explanation from him about why he believed her destiny lay with him, why he saw her as his mate, since she couldn't feel it. Watching her think was sexy. The powerful attraction he felt for her wasn't the same for her. She needed proof he couldn't give.

"Of all my brothers, it's true I've always been more attracted to vampires. It only intensifies my feelings for you, but it isn't the only reason I like you. That would be like asking me if I only talk to you because you have red hair, or am I only doing my job when I asked you to tango with me earlier?"

Flame smiled and shook his head.

"I admit to liking your red hair and doing my job, but I wanted to talk with you about more than your hair color. I enjoyed dancing with a woman who knows how."

Flame cut off that line of thought. He was a man who found her to be an attractive woman. That was enough reason to like someone.

If there came to be more reasons, then they would ice the cake, so to speak. It was enough that Hannah was curious about him. He wanted her interest. He craved her desire.

"Have you been with many vampires?"

Hannah compared herself to whatever she thought he expected. She didn't have experience. She lacked in her dating skills all the confidence she had in the dance. Hannah felt inadequate because she lacked experience.

He could help her move past it. Flame needed her to see him for the man he was, not the image his charisma led most to believe. She had no competition from any woman, living or dead, past or present. None held a candle to the fire which burned in him for her.

"No. Would you know my past?"

He had even less experience than she probably had in relaying the past. He had no confidence in sharing anything with another, and he was near-certain parts of his truth might push her away.

If she'd ever accept him as her mate, he wanted to make sure she knew everything. He needed to be the first one she heard it from. It needed to be the truth, or he had no chance with her.

"I would know it if for no other reason than you know mine."

It was her sincere choice, and she had a valid reason. He wished to deny her nothing.

"Six hundred and twenty-nine years ago, a Norse ergi sedr shaman resurrected me as a dragon. He was a skilled necromancer, and the Ri ruirech of Leinster had asked him to make dragon protectors of the realm. I was a lord of my castle in my former life as Diarmuid Cinead. I died defending my home. He pulled my soul from the underworld into this realm. He tethered it to this dragon. I became Flame."

He stood and walked a few paces away. Flame struggled with speaking the truth to her. She needed to hear it. He needed her to know his story, no matter how reticent he was to share the tragedy of his existence.

"I have only a handful of memories from my life as a man. The shaman left me my face and my name, but he broke me as a man. Much as you were."

He whispered it. That was difficult to recall.

When he had control again, he turned back to face her. She nodded her understanding of his need to say it and then move past it. Likely as not, she wanted to compartmentalize the similar recent episode in her life.

"I swore the required fealty and service oaths to the Ri ruirech and my riders. As a dragon, assigned to a Ruiri, life was good at first, I guess. I'd always enjoyed the feast, the wedding, the winter solstice celebrations, and the parties. I remember a party where I danced with a beautiful redheaded woman from my life as a lord. My Ruiri and I had a good relationship when I became a dragon. I attended many social functions with him as his dragon knight. I was as a dragon what I had been as a man. But mortals die."

Flame paused. Remembering what happened next was difficult.

"The next Ruiri wasn't a moral man, but I served. Several years into his rule, we lay siege to the castle of a Ri tuaithe, one of his under kings, who, although he'd agreed to give his daughter's hand in marriage to my king, later refused to keep the agreement."

"We took the castle, killed the Ri tuaithe, and my king claimed his wife. He also took the two younger sisters as captives to keep his new wife compliant with his wishes. His wife didn't survive for long as he treated her poorly. When she died, the two younger sisters were extra mouths to feed. With no family to speak for them, he thought to put them to good use. He enlisted them as dragon riders. They were only twenty and twenty-one years old. Clara was the older, and Joselle was the younger, both with red-hair and green-eyes, pretty young girls. They had lived a sheltered life. They were innocent of the ways of dragons and riders, innocent of men."

"What ways were those?"

"Sedr magic governs a dragon's ability to fly. Unbonded dragons can't fly without a rider who has a physical connection to us. The system used then required dragons to service the riders so we could always fly into battle."

Flame tried to soften the picture.

"You mean you had to sleep with them?"

Flame nodded and looked away from her, ashamed. He couldn't face the disgust he knew would mar her features.

"They were human. They would grow old and die. New women became dragon riders all the time. For some poor orphans, it became their meal ticket. All dragons are shifters. We are sterile, so there was no risk of pregnancy. I couldn't always guarantee I would have the same rider, so I served every rider who requested it from me."

"For how long?"

She understood exactly how miserable that existence could be. But she had to know the truth. If she thought he lied, her trust in him would evaporate, and he'd lose her for sure.

"Over three centuries. I could've stopped it if I'd chosen a woman and turned her into my Valkyrie, but I didn't want just any Valkyrie. You see, I can turn only one for mine. I wanted to turn my lifemate into my Valkyrie. If she wouldn't have me, then I would consider an alternative."

Flame needed her to understand why he hadn't simply chosen a woman and ended his misery. He sighed and pulled himself together. Then he told her the truth only one other living soul knew.

He breathed in. It wasn't a simple story for him to tell, even after five centuries had passed.

"I've already admitted my singular attraction to redheads, have I not?"

Hannah nodded and smiled. Flame collected his thoughts and continued.

CHAPTER NINETEEN
Understood Him

Flame

"When the two girls arrived in the barracks, I was the only dragon in residence. I alone knew what had happened to them. I couldn't allow things to proceed."

"They were innocent, and I couldn't take that from them. They begged me for help. I disavowed my orders, and I smuggled them out of the castle to Lachsmead. It was only a tower left of an ancient, abandoned castle. I saw to it they had provisions and were safe. I had a job to do, and it forced me to leave them. They preferred a ruined tower to the life of a dragon rider."

Flame swallowed the lump in his throat.

"Things were fine for weeks. I would fly out and visit them with rations and necessities. They thanked me. We talked. I'd even worked out a way to get them out of Leinster to Dublin, where a friend had promised to help them find husbands. It was all arranged."

Hannah's attention didn't waver.

"On the next visit, before they were to travel, Joselle had taken ill. There was little I could do for her that her sister hadn't done. She was dying. I stayed longer than I should have. Clara became ill next. It was horrible. Dragons aren't healers."

"What did you do?"

Hannah whispered, desperate to know, but afraid of what might happen.

It mattered that she was curious about him, his life, and his story. It soothed him. He wanted to share his life with her.

"I turned them into vjestice vampires, like you. They drank the dragon blood from my wrist. I taught them what I showed you. They lived. I taught them how to hunt. But I tarried far too long. When I returned to the castle, my week-long absence caused a stir. I lied and said I'd misjudged my flight ability with no rider and walked through the forest."

"Things went well for a while. I avoided the sisters and Lachsmead tower. But eventually, I felt compelled to check on them. I flew out to Lachsmead. My king suspected me and followed me with men on horses unbeknownst to me. They arrived before I left and caught me with the girls in the middle of the night."

Hannah drew in a breath in alarm.

"My king assumed the worst of me. He'd wanted the girls exploited. He thought I had kept them for myself. When he realized I'd turned them, he ordered my execution for insubordination, even though I'd never been denied my shifter abilities before."

Flame shrugged.

"It's true. Giving dragon blood to another in a non-life-threatening situation is forbidden. They were dying, so I felt justified in my behavior. I'd even asked them first if they would accept the dark gift from me. They could have chosen against it. I had their consent. They were of age."

Flame sighed out an old sorrow.

"My king saw it differently and left me in the Netherworld. Clara and Joselle he gave to his men. His men left them broken and bleeding for the dawn to take them."

Flame paused, closing his eyes. He hadn't known, trapped in the Netherworld as the ones he had sought to protect, suffered ruin by his king's men at arms. It broke something in him which had never fully healed.

"Dragons rise with the dawn, even if we die. We lose our memories, though. An hour in the Netherworld is a day of this life lost to us. Confused, when I came back, I couldn't find them, even though I searched everywhere. I couldn't remember what happened. When I returned to the castle, I reported for duty. I served my king, but my heart ached."

Even centuries later, his heart still ached.

"Blaze was the one who finally took pity on me. I confessed the tale right until the last thing I remembered. He began the investigation. When he finally learned what happened, he sat me down and told me the truth. I cried like a small child. Blaze comforted me in my darkest hour. My king betrayed me."

Blaze alone knew the truth he'd just told Hannah.

"It got worse. My king told lies about how I turned the girls into my sex slaves and left them to burn. The men, who didn't know better and hadn't taken part in the debauchery perpetrated against the girls, would no longer look at me. Those who helped my king spread his lies. The king put me in the dragonsworn robes of a servant. He decided I was no longer fit to be a knight."

His grief left him silent, unwilling to defend himself.

"Ash got involved. Blaze tipped him off that something was wrong. Blaze never spoke a word against me, and he held his tongue about my story. He said it was my business. They should ask. No one did. They believed the lies."

Flame hissed. Those who should have helped him hurt him worse than what his king did.

"Ash eventually heard all the rumors and lies. He asked me only one question before he judged me unfit to continue to serve. He asked only if they'd been willing participants. I felt too betrayed and angry to defend myself. Ash removed me from the castle in disgrace. For many years, I served the Ri ruirech while Ash replaced me."

"I'm your redemption then?"

She was intelligent. Her quick mind drew him as much as her physical beauty.

"When I first saw you, I thought so. I wanted to believe you might save me from my past. That if I could somehow help you, it would right the injustice done to Clara and Joselle. But it doesn't work that way. I failed them, and I have to live with it. Whether my mate ever accepts me, I failed to protect the innocent."

"You didn't fail them. Their system failed you all. How could a man like you be in service to a king who had no problem abusing women?"

Her innocent question strangely absolved him.

Flame loved her at that moment. She defended him. She'd listened patiently, heard the entire story, and then defended his actions because she understood him as a man.

CHAPTER TWENTY

Slipped Away

Flame

She recognized the good in him instead of assuming the worst. Hannah believed him. She had taken his part. No one had ever accepted him unconditionally like she had.

"That's why I was the last dragon to be convinced to serve again. But I have hope things will be different this time. Luke is different. He's a direwolf. He's the Ri ruirech, but he leads the pack. In a pack, all the members are equal. None are a lower class or of lesser rank. Everyone works together and agrees Luke and Eli lead if a leader is required. Hell, Luke has a council to help him decide. The Ruiri, whose interests I must protect, is a bear shifter who's mated to a vampire."

"She's like me?"

Hannah's interest piqued with what she thought might be a kindred soul.

Flame smiled at her. Hannah was a vampire, and even if she claimed to be happy being a lone vampire, it wasn't true.

The nature of the vampire was sexual. The sedr magic was stronger than any other magic in them. Their gregarious need for others, to socialize, to enjoy the party, and be a part of the group, was well-documented.

Even feeding was a sexual experience for them. Well, did Flame know it. He'd never touched Clara or Joselle, but he had experienced the euphoria of the vampire's bite.

"Yes. When you have recovered sufficiently, I shall introduce you to her. She's old and powerful. They are to be raised to the Council this upcoming Saturday. Would you like to see the ceremony? I would love to take you."

"Oh, yes! I would love to see it. Where will it take place?"

Hannah became excited at the prospect of seeing the ceremony. Her interest in anything like a party or event which held pageantry was proof that part of her turning was correct, at least.

Maybe part of the attraction for him was her enthusiasm for celebratory occasions. He enjoyed the party and the social life the same as the vampire did.

"The ceremony will take place in the stone circle at Draoithe at twilight. We will go."

Time crept closer to dawn. Flame had grown tired. He could see Hannah was tired as well. It had been a long, eventful night. They needed sleep.

The dragons would meet later to debrief and review any new information. If there were new orders from Luke, Ash would let them know.

"I need to sleep. Will you drink from me?"

She looked at him for a long time, then she nodded shyly and looked away, ashamed.

"Please don't be ashamed. What happened to you isn't your fault. But if you prefer not to bite me, I can bleed for you. You can drink it from a glass if it would make it easier for you."

He wanted to feel her bite, but he felt he should offer. Would she see his desire? Did her desire compel her?

"I'm ashamed only because of the way it feels to me."

"It feels similar to the way it felt to kiss me. It's like a sexual experience. You're a vampire, a super predator. Even feeding is sexual. It needs to be for vampires to survive. Perhaps tomorrow evening, after you practice ice, fire, and levitation, we'll work with allure. It's a harder skill to master."

"Okay. Are you sure it will be okay if I drink from you?"

She preferred to bite him. Flame exalted in her choice.

"It will be far more than okay. I want it that way. I simply didn't wish to make you feel uncomfortable."

Flame grinned at her.

He shouldn't have offered, but he was as caught up in it as Flare had once been. It was an addiction he had no desire to step away from.

"Nightshade, I don't want you to feel trapped. If I learn to allow you to stop the thirst by drinking animal blood, I will help you. Until then, for as long as you will accept my protection, you may drink your fill from me at dawn. I can't give it to you more often, because I fear it."

Hannah frowned.

"Dragon blood is too powerful. Some dragons allow women to take from them at will, but it acts as a drug, destroying the mind. The women become thralls, unable to function without it. Eventually, it kills them. I can never allow that to happen to you.

Once a night at dawn is safe. It's how the Valkyries drink."

Hannah yawned. The sun called her to sleep. They walked back to the room. He turned his back to her as she dressed for bed. They lay down together. He embraced her so she could bite his neck.

He prepared for it. He preferred to be in control of himself, but he was already expecting her bite. Flame wanted it badly. His cock was already rock hard thinking about it. Her bite was as addictive to him as his blood was to her.

Flame hissed at the pain when her needle-like hollow fangs pierced his neck. When the venom burned, he wanted to jerk away. The pain was excruciating.

When she drew his blood from his body, his balls drew up in response, and he came long and slow. Flame was certain he was a closet masochist at that point.

The ejaculation matched her swallowing of his blood. They both moaned in pleasure when she finished. He knew she felt it, too. The intensity was greater than it had been before. Learning about her and sharing some of himself with her made a stronger connection between them.

The wound sealing closed, followed by a sickening feeling as her fangs receded. He rose and changed boxers. He cleaned himself and checked to see if she needed cleaning, but found no evidence. She looked at him drowsily. The dawn called.

"Thank you. You taste divine, like cognac and linen. Too rich. I feel drunk again. You feel good. Will you hold me? I want to feel safe like before. Strong arms around me. I want to drown in the feeling of you…"

Hannah slurred something about how good he smelled. Then she was gone to the sun.

He attracted her. Perhaps he had a chance with her after all.

He was too tired to stay awake, so he joined her in sleep as she'd requested. Flame tightened his grip on her so she couldn't disappear from him while he slept after pulling her to his chest. He erased the evidence of her bite, then he, too, slipped away into his dreams.

CHAPTER TWENTY-ONE

Part Of My Soul

Hannah

When she woke, it was nearly three in the afternoon. Cognac and linen surrounded her. She had slept in his arms again after getting drunk on his blood.

She had taken less from him than she had before. Maybe she didn't need it as much. That was a good thing, right? She hoped it was.

Her behavior still disgusted Hannah. All her life, she'd been in control of her thoughts and behaviors.

She was a dancer. Control and precise movements had defined her existence. Athletes relied on diligence and practice. She'd always chosen each course of action.

When Flame offered her his blood, she'd followed him, practically salivating. He was like a drug she could not say 'no' to. She didn't want to be an addict.

It warred with her other feelings about the man. Flame had been kind and generous. He'd given her back her ability to touch the flame. She was still in awe of that. She was den lasair.

Then he'd taught her to levitate and make things hot and cold with her mind. It was wild knowing she held serious magic beyond her small fire.

Flame said she had other dark gifts. To him, what had happened to her wasn't a curse.

When she'd bitten him at dawn, it was so erotic they both moaned. He'd cum from the euphoria again as he had before. Her panties soaked through, wishing for more intimate contact with him. It was madness.

Hannah replayed the events of the previous evening in her mind. He danced with her, drank with her, kissed her, and taught her magic. Flame was charismatic, but he'd also shared some of his past with her. He said he liked her, asked her out to dance, and offered to take her to a ceremony on Saturday.

Was he serious, or merely doing his job?

She liked Flame, but Hannah wasn't sure about things. What was she supposed to do next? How was she supposed to behave? It was all new to her.

She remained skeptical. If she'd never become a vampire, she wouldn't even know who he was. Hannah barely knew him, and just because he was nice to her didn't mean he didn't have real powerful magic. He felt dangerous, but she didn't believe he was evil.

Flame was a man. She was wary of him. She didn't want to be tricked into being hurt again, and she still wanted out of her wretched situation.

One night of revelry didn't lead to resolving all of her issues. A night enjoying his company didn't give her the day. Nothing could give back the career and life she'd worked for.

Why did he have to be so damn perfect when everything about her life lay in ruins?

"Nightshade, what do you fear?"

His deep, sleepy voice was low and sexy in her ear.

Was it normal to be attracted to just the sound of a man's voice? Did it matter? Nothing was normal about her situation.

She closed her eyes and let his voice vibrate through her.

"I fear never seeing the sun again."

She told him the truth. She had no reason to lie. Hannah despaired of adjusting to her life as it now was.

What had he said? Was she fading? Is that what was happening?

"Would it truly be so terrible to you to never see it?"

He could not fake his seriousness.

"No more sunrises, no more sunsets. Never again to see a butterfly on a rose or a hummingbird drinking from a morning glory at dawn. It might be. I long to see the mist rise over the ocean with the morning sun. I miss coffee as the sun rises."

Hannah didn't hide her sadness.

"There's a way to see the sun again, Nightshade. It would be painful, and you'd be bound to that new life as surely as you're bound to this one now. Consider if it's truly worth the sacrifice you'd have to make, then if you ask me for it, I can give you back the sun."

"You could do that? You could make me not be a vampire? I could be just me again?"

Hannah held all the hope the dream had. Her desperation to have her life back was pitiable. He shook his head sadly.

"No. No one can do that. You'll always be an immortal vjestice vampire, and you'll have to face eternity. They added you to the Leaindeail. These things I can't remedy. But I have the power to transform you into a Daywalker. There's a heavy price. It's beyond painful to one such as you, and it would be permanent. Weigh it carefully."

Flame offered her something different, but there would be no take-backs. She didn't want to hurt anymore. Maybe later she could think about it.

She'd always be a vampire. She should learn it well then. If she had no other life left, then her vampirism needed to be embraced, right?

"How long is the offer good for?"

"For as long as I exist. There's no need to choose now."

So he gave her an option for a future time. Maybe she couldn't live in the dark. If not, she could reconsider it.

"I'll think about it. If I must always be a vampire, then maybe I need to learn that first."

Hannah sighed, resigned.

She rose to prepare herself for the day, only to realize it wouldn't soon be night. The sun trapped her indoors for several hours before nightfall would free her. Hannah needed to reorder her life.

Hannah went to the chest, removed undergarments, and opened the wardrobe to choose clothes. They weren't her clothes.

Nothing of her familiar life remained. Her tears leaked from her eyes. She tried to sniff them back when she remembered they'd stain anything they touched with blood. It was hard not to mourn her losses.

Flame had her wrapped in his arms instantly. He'd been studying her, watching her reactions. It was sweet of him to ease her depression.

Cognac and linen eased her mind. He could do that. He could steal her distress. Did she want that? Maybe she needed to feel it. Taking it from her didn't let her work through it.

"Flame, I need a shower."

She spoke to his hard chest.

"Will you be okay if I let go?"

She wanted to stay locked in his powerful arms forever. She could let him love her and banish the old nightmare, but it wasn't real.

"I need to work through it. If you steal it from me, I can't figure out how I feel. Please?"

Flame let her go immediately, albeit reluctantly. Flame couldn't ease some things. He knew that.

For some things, a person had to deal with them, compartmentalize them, and move past them.

"I will be here if you need a sounding board."

Flame turned to his clothes. He needed to dress and start his day, too. He opened the wardrobe and fingered a long stick. It was a spear which appeared old and worn. He was about to push it aside and withdraw his clothes, but as Flame seemed willing to answer her, she asked about it.

"What's that?"

Flame grabbed it and brought it out.

"Please don't touch it. But you may see it. It could harm you if you touch it."

Hannah moved to look at it closely. It drew her to it. She could feel the magic in it. It was wooden, stained, and covered in strange carvings.

Oddly enough, it felt faintly like Flame. When she looked closer, the carvings glowed. Flame became alarmed and pulled it back from her a bit.

"What is it? Why does it glow?"

Hannah looked up at him for answers.

"It's a life spear. My life spear. This spear was used to make me into a dragon. If I'm to be destroyed, this spear will be the way I die... forever. Grey dragons can't handle iron weapons without incapacitating pain. This spear has been through many battles with me. As I'm invincible, so is it. It returns to my command. I can't give it up unless I give my life to my Valkyrie. Then it will answer only her command and mine. She alone may destroy me. Only another dragon or a Valkyrie may touch it without harm. It glows because you are *den lasair*. It responds to your command of the flame."

"It knows what I am?"

A stick entranced Hannah. Perhaps she'd lost her mind, but something about the stick drew her in and captivated her. She itched to touch it. But she refrained. She wanted no more pain.

She had her fire back and his fire felt clean. The magic in the spear felt darker. Best to leave it alone. His nervousness was enough to warn her away.

"The part of my soul which touches the dragon fire is bound to the spear. It recognizes the ability to touch the flame in you. The magic which the O'Keefe women have is the same magic the necromancer used to give the dragons their flames. I'll die without my fire. It's how the shaman started my heart. I'm sadly nearly positive someone stole an O'Keefe woman's magic to create my brothers and me."

"You mean someone murdered her for her flame?"

Flame nodded his belief.

"It's what makes you feel dark and edgy to me, isn't it?"

Trying to understand the dream was difficult. Magic, she accepted, but never had she thought it could be so complex.

"Yes, and it's why dreamwalkers dislike grey dragons. We aren't in the dream properly. Some, like Kallik, are skilled enough to use the dream as second sight. We appear as ghosts to them. Vampires have difficulty teleporting dragons because we don't travel the dream properly, either. The spear contains a part of my soul."

CHAPTER TWENTY-TWO

The Greatest Treasure

*H*annah

"Vampires can teleport?"

Could she teleport?

"If they take a consort, yes. It magnifies their magic, and they can teleport anywhere they're familiar with. The place has to be safe from the sun, but it eases travel restrictions during daylight hours."

"I need a shower, but I have ten million questions."

DARK CURSE

Flame put the spear away.

"I need food. What would you like to do about the questions?"

"How about you join me to wash up? It worked yesterday. Then I'll have tea while you eat breakfast at three in the afternoon, and I'll ask you ten million questions. What do you think?"

Hannah smiled at him. She needed to learn. If Flame allowed it, she needed answers. He sighed in relief.

"Thank you. I almost died leaving you for three hours yesterday. My blood demands I be near you. It presses me remorselessly. As long as I'm in your presence, I still function. It felt as if my heart wanted to leap from my chest and run back to you the entire time I was away."

"You're suffering to let me drink from you!?"

Hannah couldn't believe it. She forced him to suffer, so she didn't thirst. That was all kinds of wrong. Her distress increased. She didn't want to cause him a problem. He helped her.

"No man who thrives in the presence of a beautiful woman is suffering. You see things wrong. My mission is to help you, and my heart desires to make you safe and comfortable. My magic even responds to you. Everything about you lights my world. I'm not suffering so long as you allow me your presence."

Flame laughed, a genuinely joyful sound as they moved out of the room and down the hall to the bathroom.

"I have control of my magic, mostly. As long as I don't go too far from you, it's not a problem."

Hannah shook her head in disbelief. Flame was as crazy as she was.

Knowing he was as captivated by her as she was by him made her heart beat faster. Hannah admired him. Maybe secretly drooled over him was a better description. Every time they talked, every time she learned more, the worse her attraction to him became.

"If you prefer to shower, I can shave and brush my teeth first."

When they stepped into the bathroom, Hannah nodded at Flame's suggestion.

He was kind enough to give her his back so she could disrobe and step into the shower. She put the water too warm, but the fire in her had always liked it that way.

She shampooed her hair and washed quickly. She shut off the water and wrapped a towel around herself before she stepped out of the shower and wrapped her hair in a second towel.

DARK CURSE

Flame grinned at her when she stepped out.

"I will never take advantage of you, Hannah. But I have to tell you how beautiful you are. Only a fool could avoid seeing that."

Hannah blushed and stepped away from the shower so he could have it.

As soon as he closed his eyes to wash his dark auburn hair, she let the towel drop and hurriedly dressed. When he stepped out of the shower, she stood before the sink, brushing her teeth.

"Hannah, do you brush your fangs, too?"

She looked up into the mirror and almost choked on the toothbrush as she watched him dry off. He was a gorgeous man. His reddish-brown hair color repeated itself in the trail down the hard sections of his abdomen to the fur surrounding his masculinity.

When he lifted one leg toweling off, his balls hung heavily in the space between his legs. The necromancer must have been in love with men because Flame was perfect.

His masculinity was noteworthy. He wasn't even hard, and really? How could a man be so well-endowed?

He looked up when she didn't answer and caught her staring at him in the mirror. Flame grinned as he stood up. He held the towel out away from himself and held his arms out for her to see him.

He turned around slowly in front of her. Flame let her look. She noted the water droplets he'd missed with the towel on his left shoulder blade and the ones on his right hip. He dripped water on the leg he hadn't toweled yet.

The dimples on his back, just above his perfect ass, were even sexy. Hannah took advantage and ogled him for the entire spin.

He was drop-dead gorgeous. Narrow waist, muscled arms, and v-shaped torso. His back looked as if she should pant after him as he walked away.

When Flame faced her again, she remembered herself, blushed, and looked away from the mirror. He laughed as he dressed. He wasn't shy.

Hannah finished brushing her teeth and combed out her damp hair. She left her red tresses down this time. They were curly, but she didn't care. She didn't wish to dry it in the afternoon heat.

When Flame dressed, he remained as sexy as he had been naked. Hannah caught her breath. He distracted her.

She had trouble thinking when he was too close. She wasn't sure if she should feel so attracted to him. Did drinking his blood do that?

It hadn't been that way with the nameless ones. They'd never given her enough blood to stop the thirst, either. They'd hurt her. Flame helped her.

He opened the door, and they stepped into the hall, making their way toward the dining room as she puzzled out her desire for Flame.

"It's okay with me if you want to look, Hannah. If you like what you see, that's even better."

"I'm not comfortable with it."

"You're so athletic. You're telling me you never had to dress or undress in a mixed company for a routine you were performing?"

"That was different. I never saw them that way."

His pursuit of the most uncomfortable topic left her exasperated.

"Never saw them in what way?"

"As attractive or desirable."

She clapped both hands over her mouth, embarrassed, as he laughed. Her face flushed bright crimson.

"It's nice to know it's mutual, then."

He chuckled as they stepped into the dining room. He admitted his desire for her yet again, but as always, he did nothing but state it.

The countertop overflowed with dishes of cooked food. Flame went to the fridge to get some tea. He slyly poured the blood from the pitcher down the drain and rinsed both the pitcher and the sink before placing the pitcher in the dishwasher.

Hannah found a plate and served him the meat and cheese with several rolls.

Flame raised his brow when she handed him the plate, but he didn't remark on it. He sat and ate it all, then went back for one more plate. He still didn't serve himself any vegetables.

"You don't eat vegetables?"

"Not usually. The occasional potato or ear of corn. Bread is good, but mostly meat and cheese. Dragons develop excellent rapport with the local butcher. All of my brothers and I like to hunt as well, but we kill nothing we don't eat. None of us eat reptiles either. It feels wrong."

Dragons were carnivores then. She'd never liked meat much. She wasn't a vegetarian. Salad and vegetable soups had become her staple diet if she wished to maintain her athletic build.

It seemed she no longer had to consider that anymore. Blood, apparently dragon blood, and specifically, Flame, was the only thing on the menu.

She ignored the line of thought. The disgust mixed with desire was too much to deal with. Besides, she couldn't taste him except at dawn.

"Flame, can you explain to me what you mean when you say a vampire takes a consort, or a shifter takes a mate? I know there's sex involved, but when you say it, I feel like there's much more to it than an 'I do' and a honeymoon."

Flame laughed.

"Immortals don't marry. If one's mate or consort dies, it kills the other. So there can be no death-do-us-part. We don't intend any parting. For shifters, the intensity of the attraction to one another slowly increases with the bond. It doesn't plateau or fade as it can for human partners. That's why finding you was like finding the greatest treasure of all time."

CHAPTER TWENTY-THREE

Dark Curse

*H*annah

"There's magic involved. How does it work?"

If she could embrace life as an immortal vampire, she needed to learn. The Leaindeail wasn't a place she understood. Immortals and magic weren't things with which she had great familiarity. The rules all seemed strange.

"Sedr magic presents many complexities. I've been studying it for centuries. Blaze and I are probably the only dragons who hoard old scrolls and manuscripts dealing with that kind of magic. Honestly, I wanted to pick his brain on some issues which bother me about your particular case, but that's off-topic."

Flame frowned, redirecting his words to focus on her query.

"Let me explain about vampires because it's the topic you need the most knowledge of first. Sedr magic in a vampire is stronger than any other magic they may possess. You can change your guise, and your ears will be a bit more pointed. Your eyes will bleed red away from the pupil, you will show your fangs, and the nails on your hand will become claws. That's basic shifter magic. It grants immortality, but it's underdeveloped in the vampires. Your transformation with magic granted you limited control over fire, ice, and levitation. But it's the sedr magic which dominates. Without its strength, the other magic would destroy you. Sedr magic drives your allure and lets you take a consort. Add in veritas magic and you can seal yourself to another, cast spells, and teleport through the dream."

Flame looked up at her to see if she followed his explanation. She nodded. She had magic. Hannah had used it yesterday. She'd always had a flame. so while she had never known more than a blurred peripheral edge of his world before the nameless ones, Hannah wasn't clueless.

Who knew being a nerd was so sexy? Maybe it was the masculine package the information came wrapped in, but Flame was smart and it was a serious turn-on.

"Everything about a vampire lures others to them. The way you look, the way you speak, your scent. The way you feed is even sexual. Vampires are the ultimate sexual predators. For a man to resist a vampire who is actively using allure against him requires a supreme effort. Most vampires enjoy their allure and use it in sexual play with other vampires who aren't immune to it. Few vampires take consorts, truthfully."

"When a vampire finally takes a consort, the male has to be virile. For the sedr magic to combine the souls as consorts, a lot of energy has to be produced from the male, and the female has to accept the male's dominance of her sexually in every way a man can dominate a woman. The magic requires the man to satisfy the female's desires sexually, no matter what they are. The law of three is prevalent in sedr magic."

Flame waited for her to consider what he said.

"Do you mean he has to take her all three ways?"

Hannah couldn't quite bring herself to say it any other way. She appreciated how he explained in the third person as if two people she didn't know in a pornographic film were involved. But it didn't stop her from feeling embarrassed or from imagining the two participants were Flame and herself.

"Yes, exactly. Before they begin, they have to exchange blood to start the consort bond between them, and when he finishes, they have to exchange blood again to bond their souls together as immortal lovers."

"It sounds romantic, but why would anyone do that?"

"Some vampires do it to gain the ability to teleport. The weaker one, usually the female, becomes dependent on the stronger one, usually the male. He becomes her source, and she drinks only from him every morning at dawn. He hunts for himself to feed her because she submits herself to him, and he usually claims her magic for his own."

Flame waited for her to once more think it through and connect the dots.

"So a powerful man could force a woman to be his consort, even if she didn't want it? Not romantic, just about power."

She surmised the truth quickly enough. Flame nodded in confirmation of her summary. It was often rape and subjugation instead of sex and love. Vampires must play a nasty game of power politics. Hannah wanted no part of it.

"Not that all vampire consortiums work that way, but it's often the case. Not here. Kallik is Mihaela's consort. He's zduhaci bound, her source, but he gives his strength to her, instead of taking hers for himself. She's in love with the big bear, and he never seizes her magic for himself. He doesn't need it. He's a powerful and highly skilled dreamwalker. His not being a vampire was likely a draw for her."

"What about the other two vampires here?"

Hannah wondered about others like herself. If they could live as vampires, maybe she could do it, too. If Mihaela had a zduhaci-bound blood source, then maybe Hannah could have one.

Would Flame be zduhaci bound to her if she asked? If she had a zduhaci, could she get her life back?

"Andrei is a mate-consort to Nadine. Ryker fell for the panther who killed him, and she claimed him for herself. Vampire magic is weaker than shifter magic, so both men drink only from their mate consorts. Rumors claim Andrei is the fastest vampire alive. He runs with his eagle when she flies every night. Ryker is partly a panther. When he became zduhaci unbound, he had the blood of the panther in his mouth. She'd bitten him, and even as a human, he bit her back."

Flame smiled and shook his head. That sounded like a long, involved story.

"What about Mihaela? What's she like?"

Hannah wanted to know about the female vampire. Would the female vampire help her? Would she know a way to reverse her current situation? She believed Flame, but maybe another vampire could help her more.

"She's a beautiful Romanian woman, long, flowing, black hair, black eyes."

"Like mine?"

"No. She was born with hers. They bleed red when she shifts guises."

Flame answered her, even though his answer wasn't what she wanted to hear.

"What else?"

"She chose her consort well. Kallik makes her happy. She was lonely as the Princess of a small enclave. For sure, she's over four centuries old and powerful. She looks to be your age, though. She's royalty and people have treated her as such for all the years she has been a vampire, but she's kind-hearted and loyal. Mihaela had no fear of a few dragons when we first met. I think perhaps you'd like her. I'll speak with Kallik about arranging a meeting."

Flame either had a serious thing for vampires, or Mihaela was really beautiful. That she had black hair eased Hannah's mind. Flame had a thing for redheads.

Hannah grew aggravated with the jealous line of reasoning. Flame didn't belong to her. He wasn't her dragon. Why should she care who he looked at?

"Why not just ask Mihaela?"

"I'm unbonded, and she's everything to Kallik. He wouldn't appreciate it if I approached her. He's a bear shifter. They're rather possessive of their mates. He'll deny her nothing, however. I'm supposed to be protecting Kallik's interest at Draoithe. He ordered me to protect her instead. He is a pacifist, but he killed two men from within the dream when they tried to take her away from him. I've no wish to be mistaken for the third such fool."

Flame laughed as if it were hilariously funny.

"I don't think murdering two people is funny."

"They kidnapped his lifemate and made it to Midland, TX, before he caught up with them. They intended to sell her to Elliot in Pecos at sunset. Trust me. They deserved what Kallik did to them. I laughed at my paranoia that my king would kill me. I suppose I should be okay with being executed. It wouldn't be as if it had never happened to me before."

DARK CURSE

Flame laughed again. This time she heard the hysteria in it, along with the hilarity. He was a dragon. Killing him set him back in time mentally. It did nothing to alter him as a dragon.

She had to assume he'd feel the pain and fear even so. His king before had executed him over vampires. He likely had no desire to be executed over the same thing by his new king again.

"Do you fear Kallik then?"

Hannah was curious. If Flame feared his king, perhaps she should avoid him.

"No, I fear little, except you. You alone of everything in the entire dream have the power to destroy me."

Flame sighed.

"Kallik is someone I ponder. Blaze convinced me if I served this time, things would be different. I swore, but I'm not collared by my king. If I choose not to swear at the Winter Solstice, I'll be free. If I choose, I could simply walk away from Draoithe and serve no more. I have no desire to suffer abuse again. If things aren't different, then I was fine with living as a man. I don't feel the need to be in dragon form as much as Char or Blaze. They need it in their souls, but I much prefer a social life. I enjoy the party too much to wreck it with my dragon."

"You would rather be just a man, not a dragon?"

Hannah was confused.

"Nightshade, I'm always a dragon. I could never be just a man, even if I wanted to. Even when I couldn't shift forms, I rescued you, and it didn't stop me. I'm an invincible immortal in whichever form I'm in. You'll likely not appreciate this as I do, but drunken bar fights in my current form are far more fun than when I shift into my dragon. My dragon scares all the fun away. Sadly, I'd have to fly in those tin cans people refer to as airplanes, but I'll survive."

He grinned at her as he stood and rinsed his plate in the sink.

Flame was hard to understand. She wanted to see him interact with other people. She longed to leave the house and walk across the grass to the little gazebo. Maybe meet more of the people Flame spoke about. How long before the sunset?

Claustrophobic levels of cabin fever grated on her psyche. What had happened to her still felt far more like a ***Dark Curse*** than any kind of gift, so long as the sun trapped her inside.

Sneak Peek at Dark Oath - Vampire Tears

Hannah

"How would you like to work? I haven't practiced since Friday. My hands itch to handle the stave."

Hannah smiled. How long since she'd practiced anything? A workout felt like a slice of her old life.

"I need to borrow a couple of practice staves. If I'm not practicing alone, I don't like to use my spear. Can you wait here for a few minutes? I think I know where to get a couple."

He pulled out his phone and was texting someone. He got a response almost immediately.

Maybe she could organize all the new information. Hannah nodded.

"I'll be right back."

He searched her eyes for something. She smiled at him.

Flame reached out to her and squeezed her shoulder with great longing in his eyes. He didn't wish to part from her.

It surprised her he left her. But he could leave the house. She couldn't leave for several hours. And a workout sounded like an excellent idea.

In jeans and boots, he left running before he even slipped out the door.

Hannah slid around the corner, away from the sunlight. It would burn before it killed her.

For a moment, she got lost in the memories. Two of them held her on the floor next to where the light streamed in through the window.

The third one laughed as he shifted the drapes to let the light touch her skin. She writhed in agony as the light burned and blistered her.

The smell of scorched flesh putrefied the air. Her hair burned on the back of her head. She lay face down on the concrete. Her back blistered, and she doubted her arm had any flesh left.

Hannah couldn't stop them. They could take what they wanted. Why did they torture her?

The sun had burned her, stopped, then burned her again. The pain was unrelenting.

"Say you want my cock, and the sun won't touch you again."

She'd obediently said she wanted it, but she didn't. The one holding her legs fumbled with his pants. He took her.

She couldn't stop him. They always made her ask for it. She always did, but she never wanted it.

The pain from the sun was almost as bad as the rape. When he finished with her, she could barely move, delirious from the pain and blood loss. Her rectum bled from the misuse.

Hannah knew she was bleeding because she could smell the scent of lavender. She passed out before the second man finished. She didn't know if the third one took his turn, but she thought he did.

Hannah woke when the water poured over her. It stung all her open wounds. It was close to dawn.

She was back in the darkroom where the light couldn't touch her. One man flipped her onto her back. Her scream of agony as the rough concrete ripped more of her flesh free echoed around the small room. The men laughed.

"Open your mouth," one man ordered her.

Hannah complied. She didn't want to, but her body betrayed her again. One by one, they slit their wrist and gave her blood to drink. She drowned in it. She swallowed fast to get as much as she could. It wasn't enough, but the thirst no longer howled at her.

They left her, locked her in, and the sun called her to sleep. When she woke, it was as if none of her suffering from the previous night had happened.

As far as she could tell, her body had fully healed. The thirst rose rapidly, though, and she despaired of ever getting out of her situation, of ever being free again.

Hannah had slid down the wall of the hallway and curled into herself as the memories overtook her. Maybe she overrated seeing the sunlight. She trembled, and the memory slowly faded as she realized someone spoke to her.

Hannah looked up to find a man who looked like Flame, but with grey hair and pale blue eyes, looking down at her. He said something to her, but she remained partly lost in her nightmare memory.

He extended his hand to help her to her feet. The man smelled of bourbon and oak. He would taste good, but she wasn't thirsty.

He was a dragon and must be Flame's brother.

Hannah was confused. Although handsome, he frightened her, and she didn't want to take his hand. She didn't want the man who looked like Flame and smelled nice to help her. She wanted Flame.

The man before her did nothing to ease her anxiety. Hannah needed Flame. She shook her head at the 'look-a-like'. She hoped he'd go away.

The man who looked like Flame frowned down at her. She cringed back against the wall. Then he moved rather quickly down the hall. She could breathe again.

Flame had pushed his brother away from her rather roughly. Flame knelt in front of her. He looked at her. The other man said something to Flame. He seemed angry.

*****

Flame

"She was fine when I left her. What did you do? Did you touch her?"

Flame's demand held a sharp hiss. He felt his magic extend to comfort Hannah, but it lent power to his words as well.

"Nothing. No, I didn't touch her. I found her like that. I just asked her if she was okay and offered her a hand up. That was when she cringed away from me. Cut it out, Flame. I don't have to confess to you. You go too far."

"Go handle your own shit and stay away from mine. Your meddling will get you killed."

Nightshade was all that mattered to him. Flame would kill Smoke if he'd caused Nightshade any harm.

"Are you threatening me?"

Smoke's tone had grown angry as well.

"If you felt the need to ask, then you knew it for what it was. Back off, or I will kick your ass right here in the hall without even leaving a mark on the walls."

Flame could easily best Smoke physically. Flame only outranked Smoke because Smoke existed before him and had accumulated more magic. Few, but maybe Eldur, had Flame's skill with the staff.

"I think your shifter magic is running much too high, or I'd take you up on it. It's been a while since I whipped your ass."

Smoke grumbled and headed down the hall. Only in Smoke's dreams would that ever happen. Flame ignored his brother.

"Hannah, are you hurt?"

Flame looked at her, checking her over for any signs of wounds or bruises.

"No. I saw the sun when you left, and I had to get away from them. They would use it against me. It burns, Flame. I miss it, but it hurts me."

Hannah whispered the last as if she were physically in pain. Her anguish twisted in Flame's soul.

The sun burned her. He didn't want to know how she knew. Flame caught her up to him and held her while she sobbed. He let her cry it out. Ash stopped in the hall before he tripped over them.

Give me a minute. She had a bit of a breakdown.

Flame opened the link between himself and Ash.

I need food anyway. The chainsaws will be here shortly. There's an oak tree in the floor blocking Ember in. We'll have to cut it out.

Flame could hear the amusement in Ash's mental voice.

He stroked Hannah's hair

Why is there an oak tree in the floor?

Flame felt compelled to ask. It was a decided 'What the Fuck?' moment.

Flower decided he belonged to her. She had a paranoid, delusional fit someone would take him from her and blocked the door. She's too exhausted to take it back. Ember has agreed to pay for the entire mess... with a smile! He refuses any other intervention. I think the dragon has fallen head over heels for his earth elemental.

Ash explained the situation with a bemused look on his face.

It was about time something made him smile. Did his face crack?

Flame wondered who would get the payout on the bet.

Ember rarely smiled or made any other facial expression. They kept a running bet on when he would smile again.

I stepped back from the window. I didn't know the man had human teeth. Someone will be happy to speak with Lightning on the payout for the wager.

Ash stepped back into the dining room, and Flame smiled as he held Hannah. His youngest brother had smiled only about five times in six hundred years.

If Flower made Ember smile, Ash should let her build oak trees wherever she damn well wanted them. Ember rarely showed any emotion. Six months trapped in solitary confinement had changed the man.

Hannah pushed away from him. He needed a fresh shirt. Maybe he needed to switch to maroon. The white ones couldn't withstand vampire tears.

Want More From The Dream?

That you have read one of my stories is humbling to me. I sincerely hope you enjoyed your experience in the dream. Please be kind and leave an independent author an honest review. Your words about my stories help other readers decide to read in the dream as well and support the creative efforts of one self-publishing tiger. Thank you, -OK

OPHELIA KEE

Magic Scroll

Join the **Newsletter** for Behind-the Scenes Updates, Exclusive Offers, Sneak Peeks, and Free Stories!

Please Safelist **opheliakee@opheliakee.com**

Newsletter Friends

Support an independent author and subscribe to **Read the Draoithe Saga** and read it all before the books publish, while I write and edit, and get all the extras, such as AI audio, character art, lexicons, graphics, videos, and more.

Read the Draoithe Saga

Visit **OpheliaKee.com** for books, audiobooks, e-boxed sets, blog posts, videos, miniseries, the suggested read order, to join the newsletter, and subscribe to Read the Draoithe Saga.

OpheliaKee.com

Welcome to the dream...

Also by Ophelia Kee

Kingdom Rising
Thread
A Pack Forms
Druid Fox
Big Bad Wolf

Royal Council
Arctic Fox
Vampire Knight
Dream Walker
Vampire Panther
Angry King

Valkyrie Riders
Quest for the Valkyries
Raven's Rescue
Lord of Dragons
Nephilim's Claim
Dungeon Master
Sorceress Valkyrie
Dark Curse
Dark Oath
Dark Gift
Icy Burn
Electric Storm
Love Eternal

Shadowed Dreams
Still Waters

Crimson Dragon
Ruler of the Mind

Apocalypse Denied
Synner & Sainte

DARK CURSE

Devil's Sins
Four Horses
Reaper's Debt

Lyons Gate
Druid Ancestry
Ruined Lion
Ghostly Kingdom
Elysian Fields
Druid Dragon
Nightmare Escape
Darkest Desire
Deepest Ardor
A Conversation With Dragons

Mystic Dark Prequel Trilogy
Haunted Echoes
Ruined Hearts
Shattered Souls

Mystic Dark
Grim Dark
Kiss Dark
Dream Dark

OPHELIA KEE

Lunar Dark
Nightmare Dark
Soul Dark
Blood Dark
Godless Dark

Gods of the Dream
<u>Unlikely Kings</u>
<u>Lost One</u>
Master of Destiny
Forest Lord

Acknowledgments

Thanks, everyone!

I want to say thanks to my mom for always supporting me.

Thanks to my sister who has always been my first beta reader.

Thanks to my dragon for encouraging a tiger to play with books.

Thanks to my lost wolf, who provided inspiration.

Most of all, thanks to my readers who always ask the hard questions, which means I have to write more stories.

I love you, -OK

Contact Ophelia Kee

ARC READERS WANTED

Drop by and say hello!
*Email the author: **opheliakee69@gmail.com**

*Ophelia Kee on Social Media: Look for me on these sites.

YouTube * Threads * Facebook * Instagram * Pinterest * X

I look forward to hearing from you. Sincerely, -OK

About the Author - Ophelia Kee

Not who everyone thinks she is.
The product of someone's imagination.
The end result of a lifetime wishing to get out.
Do not buy the lie.
If you live in fear, you give up freedom.
Taking the risk and making the leap.
Too much of anything is a bad thing.
Innuendo floating on mist rising above water.
Walk away and leave it all behind.
Telling the story that haunts a fantasy.
Catching a dream.
She does not exist.
-Ophelia Kee

OPHELIA KEE

Ophelia Kee

Milton Keynes UK
Ingram Content Group UK Ltd.
UKHW021041031224
452078UK00010B/568